World Without Love

A Collection of Short Stories
That Together Tell a Story

DALLAS DOCTOR

Truffle Press   ~   New York

First Edition, May 2013

Library of Congress Cataloging in Publication Data
Doctor, Dallas, 1953-
World Without Love
A Collection of Short Stories that Together Tell a Story
p.   cm.
ISBN-10: 0615807461
ISBN-13: 978-0615807461 (GoScienceGo)

Printed in the United Sates of America

Truffle Press

World Without Love

A Collection of Short Stories
That Together Tell a Story

For Susan

TABLE OF CONTENTS

~

PART TWO

ACKNOWLEDGMENTS

Jennifer Quinn helped me with this project more than she knows. Her insights were invaluable. Her questions were relevant and thought-provoking. Her time and interest made these stories better. Her guidance is much appreciated.

Jon Mark Lundell, Bo Bradly, Vaughn Garner, Jack Redemption and Susan Hamilton all read early versions of the manuscript and provided excellent and valued feedback.

Thank you.

Preface
Viva Zapata

There used to be a seriously great bar in the 900 block of Duval Street in Key West called Viva Zapata. Don't look for it; it's not there anymore. Viva Zapata served the world's most flavorful home-made salsa and boasted the best jukebox in the history of ever. My dear friend Don Wilson and I spent many happy hours there downing dollar drafts, dipping just-baked tortilla chips into scrumptious salsa, and impressing each other with our nuanced understanding of the meaning of life.

One very late night, Don Wilson let slip that he had just finished re-reading *Great Expectations*. I responded that I had been forced to read Dickens in high school, but now that I was an adult, I only read non-fiction. (I'd been pouring over the major works of Bertrand Russell at the time and my position was that fiction was simply not rigorous enough for a mind as serious as mine.) I gleefully pointed out to Don Wilson that the terms truth and fiction were antonyms. My time on this planet, I declared, was far too precious to waste with any endeavor that often boiled down to little more than merely making stuff up.

Don Wilson said that was the most obnoxious, arrogant, and ignorant thing he'd ever heard me say. (It was the ignorant part that bothered me.) Don Wilson argued that there was more truth in well-written fiction than in all of *The History of Western Philosophy*.

The bar stools we were sitting on at Viva Zapata that night just happened to be less than half-a-city-block from Ernest Hemingway's Key West mansion, so Don Wilson reached into his bookbag and, as if by magic, pulled out a collection of Hemingway short stories along with a copy of *Great Expectations*. He handed them both to me, and made me promise to read them.

Don Wilson was right.

I was wrong.

I've been a reader ever since.

That was almost twenty-five years ago and I'm still not ready to write fiction – all of these stories are true – even the parts I made up. But in the pages that follow, I have endeavored to expose a few specific (sometimes graphic) truths, and to explore those truths for the meanings they may convey. If these stories were fictional, I would have made the main character less arrogant, less superficial, and less ridiculous. But I have opted instead to strive for honesty, courage and clarity. My hope is that I have provided some insight.

I don't know if I have approached the lofty standard that my friend Don Wilson often alluded to during our drunken debates on Duval Street, but I do take solace in the following non-fiction facts:

1) I now enjoy meaningful relationships with both Hemingway and Dickens. (Over the years, I've added many others to my circle of confidants, including Camus, Conrad, Kafka, Hugo, Hess, Vonnegut, Miller, Steinbeck, Twain, Joyce, Dumas, Austen, Orwell, Thompson, Bukowski, and a great many others.) And …

2) I still have the recipe for Viva Zapata Salsa committed to memory. And …

3) I have written these stories.

Introduction
Heart Of Darkness
Music & Lyrics by Dallas Doctor
©2010 Wild Moose Music (BMI)

(Verse 1)
I've been tryin' to face my fears
I'm tryin' to look at the world in its face
Without blinking, but now it appears
There's a terror that needs an embrace

(Chorus)
So let's go
And don't hold on
Let's just fall
And keep on fallin'
Just let go
The Heart Of Darkness
Is callin'
It's callin'

(Verse 2)
I've been tryin' to mine this adventure
For the kernels inside of the shells
I've been tryin' to tell you my future
Without understanding myself

(Chorus)
    So let's go
    And don't hold on
    Let's just fall
    And keep on fallin'
    Just let go
    The Heart Of Darkness
    Is callin'
    It's callin'

3

(Bridge)
When you don't know where you're goin'
What's the point in a plan?
Let the rivers all run where they will
All I'm doin' is all that I can

(Chorus)
    So let's go
    And don't hold on
    Let's just fall
    And keep on fallin'
    Just let go
    The Heart Of Darkness
    Is callin'
    It's callin'

(Tag)
I've been tryin' to face my fears

PART ONE

Going
(Summer 1956)

I didn't write this first story. I'm only retelling it because I think it explains a lot.

Evidently, way back in the summer of 1956 – the summer before my third birthday – my dad took a job as a fire watcher up in the wild mountain timberlands of northern Idaho. He climbed a tall wooden tower each day to survey the forest for telltale signs, while my mom, my baby sister and I stayed in the tent below.

One warm August night, apparently I'd had enough of this idyllic existence and just wanted to get on with my life.

So I left.

Mom and Dad didn't know what to do.

I was nowhere to be found.

Alone in the wilderness.

Darkness everywhere.

Panic.

Searching.

Nothing.

Something.

Up high on the next ridge.

Something.

What was that?

I had taken the flashlight with me.

I was still trudging along when Dad caught up to me.

"Where you going?" He asked.

"I'm going," was my reply.

"Going where?" He pressed.

"Just going."

Stopping
(Summer 1958)

Mom ran alongside while I pedaled. She'd hold the seat to keep the bicycle from leaning too far to one side or the other, while I gripped the handlebars and concentrated on going forward. From time to time, she'd momentarily lift her hand off the seat as she ran alongside. If my balance and forward progress were sufficient, the bike would remain upright and I'd be riding.

Whenever I glanced back to make sure she was there, she'd quickly place her hand back on the seat to let me know everything was going to be all right.

Sometimes she was helping and sometimes she was just running alongside. And it worked. I got faster and faster and better and better and I rode right away from her.

I pedaled off down the road and left her behind. I felt her fall away and it was exhilarating. Until it occurred to me that we hadn't talked about how to stop.

I didn't know how to stop.

I pedaled faster and faster and started calling out to her. She chased after me shouting. I pedaled faster. I didn't know what else to do. I made the corner and turned right. She followed behind, but she was losing ground.

I panicked and pedaled faster.

I made a second corner onto a street I'd never seen before and kept right on going just as hard and fast as I possibly could. I didn't know where she was anymore. I kept going. I made a third corner and a fourth corner and headed for home. I had no idea what I was going to do when I got there.

Mom couldn't help me anymore.

I had to do this on my own.

On purpose, I headed straight for the next telephone pole.

I pedaled hard and fast and hit it – straight on.

There were L-shaped iron spikes protruding from telephone poles in those days that the linemen used to climb the poles. I soared up over my handlebars and introduced myself to the lowest rusty spike on the pole.

It left a diagonal scar across my chest that I carried for the rest of my life.

The Great Yellowstone Earthquake of 1959

On August 17th, 1959, The Yellowstone Earthquake killed 28 people and registered 7.5 on the Richter scale. Without warning, the beet field behind my grandpa's house rose up, rolled around, and waved like it was liquid.

I didn't expect that.

Our half-loaded moving van started rocking, shaking, and bouncing.

Boxes and baskets came popping out like popcorn.

The ground fell from beneath me.

I reached out for something. Anything.

The shaking continued.

I was afraid the truck might bounce into me, or onto me, so I decided to try to run.

I got out to the paved road and turned toward grandpa's giant grain silos, and couldn't believe my eyes. Four massive ten-story concrete cylinders were wildly swinging back-and-forth like monstrous reeds in the wind. I was sure they were about to come crashing down.

That's when it stopped.

The usually-calm water in the irrigation canal continued splashing up onto the road.

But that wasn't the weird part; the weird part was standing there watching the road rising up and falling down as it rolled away from me, like a gigantic wave in a massive river of asphalt.

I didn't know a road could do that.

What a strange feeling. Solid became fluid. Then solid again. The planet disordered, then reordered itself, right before my eyes.

It occurred to me that maybe the world isn't at all what we think it is.

Every day after that was different from every day before, not just because the earthquake undercut my sense of solid, but also because it was our last day in Idaho.

The very next morning, we moved from the land of my ancestral heritage to an exotic place called Portland, Oregon. The earthquake wasn't the reason we moved, of course; we were in the process of packing up and getting ready to go when it hit. But it may have contributed to the unsettling feeling that I just couldn't shake during our journey to the strange, new land.

Something was wrong. Something was different.

I was worried about my bike.

"Are you sure it's on the truck?" I asked Mom every few minutes.

"Yes."

"But I didn't see it on the truck." I had my doubts.

"Don't even think about it. It'll only make you unhappy. Think about something else," she suggested.

It bothered me that she didn't seem to share my concern.

And just as I feared, when we pulled up at 9847 S.E. 48th Avenue, my bike was not there.

"I don't see my bike."

"Help or get out of the way, Kid." My Uncle Don and his helper Clyde were busy pulling boxes down from the back of the truck.

"But my bike? Where's my bike? It's not here!"

"I believe it's on the other truck – the one your dad is driving," Uncle Don testified. "He's still a few hours down the road, don't worry."

I wanted to believe him. "Do you know, for sure, that my dad has my bike?"

"Well, I don't see it here, so it *must* be with him." Uncle Don reached for the big picture frame on the top of the load.

"But did you actually see it on the other truck?" I needed something more concrete. "Did you actually see it?"

"It's not here, so that means it *must* be on the other truck."

That argument seemed to satisfy Uncle Don completely.

But It seemed pretty shaky to me.

I suspected there might, in fact, be a much more terrifying explanation.

"What if you're wrong?" I reached out for something. Anything.

"Don't even think about it, Kid. It'll only make you unhappy."

Nobody seemed to share my concern.

What a predicament!

I looked around. I didn't recognize anything at all. I had no idea what was going to become of my bike, or of me, or of any of us. It felt like the world was dis-ordering itself all over again.

I couldn't help it. I pestered him one more time.

"But how do you know?" I just wanted to cement the pieces back together. "How do you know you're not wrong?"

"I never worry about that," Uncle Don laughed. "Now either help or get out of the way."

There was no point in arguing. Either my bike was on the way, or it wasn't.

"Don't even think about it, Kid. It'll only make you unhappy."

Why was I the only one who needed something solid to go on?

The shaking continued.

City Slickers
(August 1959)

Sassy came skidding to a stop on her sparkly Schwinn Sting-ray banana-seat-bike with high handlebars and pink-and-white streamers flowing from the handgrips.

"You movin' in?" she asked.

"Yes." I saw she had playing cards clothes-pinned into her spokes. That's what made the noise like a motor when she pedaled. Cool. I had never seen that before.

"My name's Sassy. What's yours?"

"Reed."

"Where you from?" She seemed nice.

"Emmett, Idaho."

"Never heard of it," she laughed. "Where's that?"

"It's farm country," I explained, "We're going to be city slickers now. That's what all my cousins say."

"City slickers?"

"That's what they call us now. My dad got a new job, so we had to move."

"Do you go to school?" She asked.

"I'll be in first-grade when school starts," I bragged.

"Are there any other kids?" She was unimpressed. "Do you have a brother, or a sister maybe?"

"I am the oldest. I have a sister Karen who's four, a brother Layne, he's two, and my baby brother Kenn, he's going to be one. Plus my Mom is pregnant with another baby."

"Are you Catholics?"

What a funny question. "No, of course not. We're Mormons."

"Mormons?"

"The Church of Jesus Christ of Latter Day Saints." I had it memorized.

And then it hit me:

"You're not a Mormon?" I gulped.

"Nope, not a Mormon." She said it just as if it had never occurred to her to care about something so important.

I'd never met a non-Mormon before, but Sassy seemed clean and nice. "You don't go to church?" I worried.

"Yes, we go every Saturday," she replied.

"Saturday?" I was confused. "You're supposed to go to church on Sunday."

"Well, we go on Saturday. We're Seventh Day Adventists".

I couldn't believe it. Portland was strange place indeed. "Is everybody here a Seventh Day ... thing you said?"

"No, not at all," Sassy laid down her bike and pointed to the house next door. "Your neighbors are Christian Scientists. Their name is Cress. They're old, but they're nice. They have a dog. You'll like them. The people across the street are Methodists. They have two kids, but they're in high school. Two houses down, that's my house. And across from us are the Jacksons. They're Catholics. Brian is eight and I think Mary is the same as age as you."

Sassy seemed to know the whole neighborhood. But this orientation was extremely disorienting. I had heard of other religions before, of course, in Sunday School. The whole point of Mormonism was that God told Joseph Smith that all other religions were false – that's why he had to start a new one.

"What about my other next-door neighbor on this side?" I pointed, holding out hope.

"I don't think they actually go," she wondered. "I never see them go to church."

"This is bad." I said it right out loud.

"What's so bad about it?" Sassy reached down and picked up a rock and looked closely at it, as if this were just any other ordinary conversation.

"It's bad because all those other religions are false." (I thought this was common knowledge.) "The Church of Jesus Christ of Latter Day Saints is the one-and-only true religion."

"But that's what everybody thinks about their own religion," Sassy found a new rock to inspect.

"But they're wrong," I insisted. "Only the Mormon church is true."

"How do you know?" She looked up.

"I know it in my heart. I know it with all my heart." Certainly that would satisfy her.

"But that's what everybody thinks." She laughed.

"But they're all wrong." It was so perfectly obvious.

"But if they believe it, how can they be wrong?"

"Because its not true." I thought I had explained this already.

"So if people can believe something, and be wrong, how do you know what *you* believe isn't wrong?"

"Because I believe in the truth." It so simple.

"Well, did ya ever think that if somebody's wrong, it might be you?" She picked up her bike.

I didn't like Sassy so much any more. "I'm not wrong," I stomped my foot.

"How do you know?" She swung her leg back up over that sparkly banana seat.

"I just know." I stood my ground.

"Maybe everybody's wrong," Sassy shouted back over the sound of the playing cards in her spinning spokes as she rode away.

Matt and Mel
(1960)

My sister was too young to play with. Besides, she was a girl. So I invented Matt and Mel.

Lots of kids have imaginary friends, but I had two. And Matt and Mel were the best. We played army and tag and olly-olly-oxen-free and we hid from each other and from everybody else and we had a great time together.

Matt and Mel were especially good at hiding, which was understandable, given the fact that they were invisible, inaudible and imperceptible in every way.

The far-less-understandable thing about my imaginary friends was that when I invited them to dinner, my parents made room for them.

That surprised me.

We placed empty chairs at the dinner table and set plates, forks and glasses in front of the empty chairs. And no matter how much my sister complained that they weren't real, Mom and Dad both pretended that Matt and Mel were right there with us.

And we did that for quite some time at our house.

Matt and Mel became so much a part of the family that Mom and Dad even made sure to remind me to tell Matt and Mel to fold their arms and bow their heads every evening when we knelt down for family prayer.

After a while, I had to let go of Matt and Mel, because to tell the truth, it took some of the fun out of it to realize that my parents were so comfortable with the concept of imaginary friends.

It made me wonder if they had any.

The Caterpillar and the Daffodil
(Spring 1961)

We played prison ball that day at recess – hard and loud. Twenty minutes later, back in the classroom, it was silent and steamy and sweaty and smelly. It was hard to breathe and I could barely keep my eyes open. The brutal sun came crashing through the big wall of windows so hard that when I laid my hand on my notebook, the pages got wet. I just wanted to take a nap.

Mrs. Griffin gave us an assignment, anyway.

We were supposed to "... describe a flower from the point of view of a bug."

I didn't want to do it.

I didn't know what a flower looked like to a bug and I didn't care and I was too tired to think about it. It was too hot to think.

So I just sat there. I didn't write. I didn't even think about writing. I didn't know what *point of view* was supposed to mean and I couldn't think about anything other than how much I wanted to go to sleep.

My head started falling. I caught it. It fell again. I caught it again. But for how long? I couldn't put my head all the way down, like I wanted to, because Mrs. Griffin would notice that. And I didn't want to get in trouble. So I suffered.

The clock. Slowly. Sluggishly. But resolutely. Ticked.

The end of the period painfully approached. I knew I was going to be in trouble. Big trouble. What would Mrs. Griffin say if I didn't hand anything in? I had to turn in something. I didn't want her to be mad at me.

So just at the last minute, right at the final warning, I grabbed my pencil and – real fast – I wrote about a caterpillar on a daffodil and how the caterpillar crawled up the stem and got to the bulge in the stem and then to the petals and then inside to the delicate parts of the petals and I wrote it big so it would take up as much of the paper as possible.

I knew Mrs. Griffin was going to be disappointed in me, because I didn't do the assignment right. But I figured it was better than refusing to try at all. Besides, I could apologize to her later and maybe she would give me another chance to write it when I wasn't so tired and sweaty. I just hoped I could get out of the room before she read it. I told my self I would make it up to her tomorrow.

I made it home and got over being tired and was playing in the basement when just before dinner, I heard my Mom call out:

"Hey Bert, your eldest son's teacher is on the phone."

Oh! No! Mrs. Griffin was madder than I thought.

I stayed in the basement for as long as I could.

My heart was all twisted up, because I knew I was going to get yelled at. And probably punished. What was going to become of me?

After a long, long time, the pain of waiting for the inevitable call from my father grew worse and worse and worse until I decided that the pain and horror of anticipating the trouble was more unbearable than the trouble itself.

So I went upstairs.

I just wanted to get it over with.

"That was your teacher, Mrs. Griffin, on the phone earlier. She said that you wrote a story today that made her cry. You really touched her. She said she couldn't believe someone so young could be so sensitive and insightful. She wants to submit your story to be published in a magazine. I'm so proud of you."

Maybe grown-ups aren't as smart as I thought.

The Jump Start
(September 1961)

I was excited because it was my first day as a Cub Scout. I had my yellow bandana clasped perfectly in place and my patches with the den number sewed onto my sleeves. My socks were pulled up and I was ready to go.

But the car wouldn't start.

Mom tried again and again to get it going, but it wasn't working and we were going to be late. Or miss it entirely.

Mom told me to give the car a push out of the driveway so she could pop the clutch, but after it rolled down to where the street started, there was a bit of a little rut there and the car got stuck in it. I was only eight-years-old, so try as I might, I couldn't get it rolling again.

But Mom could. So she showed me how to pop the clutch. She told me to hold the left pedal down all the way to the floorboard, and then as soon as she got it rolling, to real fast, take my foot off and let the pedal pop up and that should make the engine turn over and start running.

So that's what we did. She pushed and she got it rolling. When she shouted for me to pop the clutch, I let it go. Mom was pushing so hard that when the car jerked forward, she fell hard on the asphalt and bloodied both her knees. The engine roared and the car leaped forward and took off down the road and I was driving.

Mom jumped up and ran behind waving and shouting as I made the first corner onto 49th Avenue and kept right on going. I had never driven a car before, so I didn't know how to stop one.

I had both hands on the giant steering wheel and I was peering out over it the best I could. But it's not as easy at it looks keeping a great big car in the street. I went up over a couple of curbs and tore up several neighbors' lawns and took out a number of shrubs and bushes, but somehow steered back onto the paved street just before I reached the intersection where 49th Avenue meets Logus Road.

I closed my eyes and made it straight across the intersection.

I turned and looked back and could still see Mom running behind and bleeding. Then I turned forward again to see where I was going. There was a church ahead. I didn't know what kind of a church it was, but it had a parking lot with long Oregon logs laid out to section off rows of parking spaces. So I steered for those logs.

The car lurched at the first log and bounced right up over it and kept right on going and headed across the parking lot toward the next set of logs. It occurred to me that the logs weren't going to stop the car. I had to try something else. It was only then that I realized that since letting the left pedal out made the car go, maybe if I pushed it in, it would make the car stop. So I stomped as hard as I could on the clutch.

The car didn't stop. It kept going. But the engine roared even louder and when the car hit the second row of logs, only the front tires made it over and the back ones didn't.

Mom came running up shouting for me to keep the clutch in. So I did. She got the door open and she did something with the gearshift and everything was okay – except for her hands and knees and several of the neighbors' lawns and bushes.

She drove me to my den meeting and we made it on time and only after that did she drive home to clean the blood off her legs and dig the gravel out of her knees and palms.

The Revelation
(October 1961)

Job #1 for any kid, trying to find his way in the world, is to keep an eye on the grown-ups around him. I was no different. And let me tell you, adults can do some funny things sometimes. If you pay attention, they can really surprise you.

I recognized very early on, for example, that the big people in my world placed much more importance on the things you did and said at church than the things you did or said at home, or school, or anywhere else. Sunday was special and church was what really mattered. Okay. Makes sense. God, and all. So I watched closely, memorized the words, and practiced the routines.

I thought that's what I was supposed to do.

Until one Sunday morning, after seeing adults do it hundreds of times, I felt like it was my turn. I stood up at Fast and Testimony Meeting and repeated – word-for-word – exactly the same lines I had been listening to all my life: "I know the Church is true, that Joseph Smith was a prophet of God, that David O. McKay is a living prophet ..." and all the rest. And then I sat down.

What happened next was completely unexpected.

The moment the meeting was over, the adults in the room swarmed me. They clamored to get to me. They fell all over themselves trying to shake my hand, to tell me how spiritually moved they were by my ".. powerful testimony."

Some had tears in their eyes.

"Out of the mouths of babes ..." someone said.

"The Spirit is strong in this young man and has revealed itself through his words," was the verdict of the Bishop.

I had only said the same things they already believed.

It was a revelation alright.

The Meadowlark
(Summer 1962)

The State Bird of Oregon is the Western Meadowlark. I know that because I went to grade-school in Oregon. Western Meadowlarks are songbirds with striped heads and bright yellow throats. In the countryside, you can hear them singing in the fields in the early mornings and evenings. They forage for insects and seeds on the ground and they nest on the ground too. It might be better for them, if they didn't, though. I know that because I spent many summers visiting my farm cousins back in Idaho.

I always got to stay at my Uncle Don's farm whenever we visited Idaho. Uncle Don's boy Lance was about the same age as me. The rest of the family usually had to all bunk up together at grandpa's ranch, but because I was the oldest, I got to go stay at Uncle Don's farm. I loved it there, because I was away from my parents. Plus, there was a lot to do and see. Uncle Don had cows and pigs and horses and sheep and goats and a canal with water-skippers (bugs that could walk on water). They had great big green tractors that even the kids could drive. They let me climb up and drive too. The tractors were huge and loud and powerful and bouncy and jumpy. You steered them with both your hands and both your feet at the same time. I loved staying at Uncle Don's farm.

And the food. The food was delicious. We'd gather around the big kitchen table in the morning and wait for Uncle Don to come in from milking with a giant glass jug filled up to the brim. There was always a super-thick layer of cream on top. Aunt Lula would strain it all through a cloth to get the flies and other gunk out of it and carefully separate the cream. Then she'd dish us out oatmeal from a big steaming pot and ladle a generous helping of that thick, goopy cream on all over it. We'd throw in three or four sugar cubes and shake some cinnamon on top and I defy you to find better oatmeal anywhere.

And that was just the beginning. There was also bacon – real fatty bacon right from the pig – and eggs that you had to wash the chickenshit off before you cracked them. There wasn't any coffee because Mormons don't drink coffee, but we had all the hot chocolate we could drink with little marshmallow cubes that floated on top. Breakfast was warm and hearty and plentiful. Nobody ever the left Aunt Lula's table unsatisfied.

And the other meals were every bit as splendid. Real food. Corn and carrots and onions and beans with dirt and just-churned-butter on them. Ham and beef and chicken and rabbit and mashed potatoes and yams. Apple pie and peach pie and pecan pie and home-made ice cream. My aunt Lula was the best cook I ever knew and Uncle Don's farm was heaven on earth.

I always slept more soundly at Uncle Don's farm than anywhere else, but very early one morning I was startled awake to shouting and calamity. It was still dark outside. And something was wrong.

Lance and I ran outside to see what all the noise was about. As far as I could gather, there was some problem with the electrical system in the milking barn. A bare copper wire had somehow become exposed or corroded or something. Uncle Don and Clyde hooked up the suction cups to the cows' udders, just as they did every morning, but that morning when they flipped the switch to turn the milking machine on, the first six cows were electrocuted.

When we got out to where the neighbors were already gathering to help with the emergency, Uncle Don had chained a dead cow by its hooves to a tractor, and he was dragging it out of the milking barn. As soon as he got the cow carcass free of the building, Uncle Don leapt down from the tractor, pulled out a large hunting knife and began cutting the cow's bloated udder off. It was all blood and mud and milk and meat and urine and cowshit and the sight and smell of it was seriously disturbing. I hadn't expected life on the farm to have days like this. I stood there in the black morning before the sun came up and asked Lance why they were cutting the cows' udders off. Lance said you had to drain the milk out of the cow or it would ruin the meat. I was impressed that he knew stuff like that, but I didn't want to watch anymore.

Later that afternoon, after the emergency had passed and the neighbors had gone back to their own farms, Lance showed me into the back room behind his parents' bedroom and pulled two rifles down from the wall. He handed one rifle to me. He grabbed a vest and pulled two boxes of bullets out of a drawer and placed a box of bullets in each of the front pockets of his vest.

We walked through some corn fields. We trekked up through some tall grass over a hill and then back down to where soybean fields butted up against a stand of giant reeds. We finally came to a slow-moving stream with tall cat-tails all around it. We called them cat-tails. They were ten-foot-tall reeds with fuzzy cylinders on top that looked like hot dogs and they only grew around the creeks and culverts and ditches and bogs. We hid ourselves in the cat-tails and Lance loaded the guns. And we waited.

A giant colorful pheasant suddenly flapped loudly – incredibly loudly – into the air just a few feet away and startled us. I pointed my rifle at it as it lifted off, but Lance stopped me.

"You need a shotgun for a pheasant," he explained.

"What's this, then?" I wondered.

"It's a .22," he chuckled.

"What do we shoot with this?" I asked.

"Don't know yet," he looked around, "just wait."

So we waited.

From the edge of the cat-tails where we were hiding, we had an unobstructed view of a vast soybean field. Lance spotted a small bird land near one of the leafy plants out in the field and quietly signaled to me. He showed me where it was. It was quite a ways away – far enough away that the chances of me actually hitting it were ridiculously small. Lance showed me how to line up the red dot on the far end of the rifle and whispered to me to hold my breath. I looked down the barrel and tried to follow his instructions.

I took a deep breath and pulled the trigger. The gun popped and the bird was gone.

Lance jumped up and started running. I jumped up and ran after him. We ran out into the soybean field waving our rifles in the air over our heads and Lance found it. It was a Western Meadowlark. I shot it right through its eye. I promise I didn't mean to. It was an accident. I never thought I would kill it. But there it lay. Dead. Poor little bird.

The Meadowlark was probably only trying to get something to eat. It hadn't done anything wrong. It wasn't bothering anybody. And I killed it anyway.

I was sorry.

So very, very sorry.

I wanted to take it back with all my heart.

But I couldn't.

We left it laying there in the dirt and I felt bad all the way back to Uncle Don's farm.

I kept thinking about how people always talk about hunting like it's a fun thing to do. I couldn't figure out what was so fun about it.

I never told anybody in Oregon that I killed a Western Meadowlark.

And I never went hunting ever again.

The Bad Kid
(Summer 1962)

Billy Waters was the bad kid in the third-grade. He wore hard, black, pointy shoes and he kicked you with them every chance he got. Billy sassed the teacher and terrorized the girls and smoked cigarettes behind the gym and got sent to the Principal's office a lot.

I lived in fear of Billy Waters. The only tolerable thing about third-grade was that for some reason, Billy didn't come to school most days. Whenever you did see him coming though, you knew something was going to happen – a slug or a kick or a shove – somebody was going to get it.

All I really wanted during that next summer was to be placed in one of the fourth-grade classes that did not have Billy Waters in it. And there was reason for hope. Billy never did his homework and he was absent so much that most of us thought there was a good chance he would never make it to the fourth-grade at all.

And we were right.

I was feeding the goats at Uncle Don's farm when Aunt Lula called me into the house and told me to pick up the phone. Back in Oregon, Billy Waters was swimming with his family at High Rocks on the Clackamas River. Billy jumped into the river and never came up. Billy's father went under so many times trying to save him that he drowned, too.

I didn't know how to feel. The bad kid was dead. I didn't have to worry about him anymore.

But it didn't make me happy.

Or sad either.

I knew I should feel something. I just didn't know what it was. I think I felt bad about not feeling bad.

But what surprised me most was the idea that somebody had tried to save Billy.

I couldn't understand that part.

I was only almost nine.

Billy never made it to nine. He only made it to eight – old enough to be baptized and responsible for his own sins – that's what they taught us at Sunday School. But, of course, since Billy's family didn't go to church, he never was baptized.

Not until that day in the Clackamas River.

Playing with Fire
(November 1962)

When Mom had her seventh baby, another boy (that made six boys and one girl so far and she wasn't done yet), I stayed at my friend Peter Gunderson's house while she was in the hospital. Peter was exactly six-months-to-the-day older than me. We camped out in sleeping bags in his basement. There were no walls in his basement – just a cement floor and some wooden frames for where the walls were going to be someday.

It was fun down there. We found a set of snow skis and pretended to be skiers. We found an old accordion and tried to figure out how to push the billows and the buttons and the piano keys all at the same time. We went exploring through the boxes to see what we could discover, always careful to put everything back the way we found it to cover our tracks.

"Look, I found my Dad's gas can," Peter got excited, "go get those matches over there on the bench."

"What? Why? Here they are."

"Watch this!" Peter poured a puddle of gasoline out onto the concrete floor and lit a match.

"Wait?"

He tossed the match. Blue and yellow flames leapt into being and danced. It was exciting. And scary.

I thought maybe when the gas got all burnt up the flames would go away, but the smoke started to get bigger and blacker, so Peter went and got an old rug and started beating the rug on the fire and he put the fire out.

"I didn't know you could do that." I was impressed. "Let me try."

Peter poured another puddle. And threw another match.

"Wait, let it burn for a minute." Peter handed me the rug.

When he gave me the go-ahead, I went to work on the fire. I swung the rug over my head again and again down onto the flames and they scattered and I chased them and I tried to catch them but they weren't going out. So Peter ran and grabbed an old blanket and threw it on the flames and stomped the fire out.

"You have to get rid of the oxygen," Peter explained. "The fire needs oxygen to burn."

"What am I doing wrong?"

"You were fanning the fire," Peter criticized. "You can't just wave at it. That makes it spread. You have to get rid of the oxygen."

"Show me."

Peter poured another puddle. And lit another match.

Then he set out after the fire with the rug. I could tell he was sort-of quickly laying the rug on the fire and letting it stay and smother the flames for a moment and then raising the rug and doing it again. And he got it out that time too.

"Okay, your turn," Peter handed me the rug.

"Let me start the fire this time," I negotiated. I was sure I had figured out the routine.

But I guess I poured too much gas.

The more I beat at it, the more it burned.

The rug I was swinging burst into flames and I had to let go of it.

Now we had two fires.

Peter jumped up and down on my flaming rug and tried to put it out the best he could, but while he was busy with that, the original fire rolled across the floor and the first cardboard box caught on fire.

Peter left my rug to burn and ran and grabbed that first cardboard box and tried to throw it away from the other boxes so they wouldn't catch fire too. But he threw the flaming box right into one of the wooden supports for where the walls were going to be, so while I was frantically trying to push the other cardboard boxes away from the flames, the wood supports started burning too.

That's when we ran upstairs.

I sat on the curb across the street, all by myself, as I watched the Firemen cleaning off their boots and rolling up their hoses and preparing to pull away. I was relieved to see that the house still looked pretty much the same as before – from the outside anyway. But I was absolutely thankful beyond measure that it was Peter Gunderson's father – and not my own – that I was going to have to face in a few minutes.

He called me into his room.

It smelled like smoke.

"You're not my son, but I'm going to have to spank you," he almost apologized.

"I desoive it."

I don't know why I said it like that.

I wasn't trying to be funny or flip or make light of the situation. I wasn't. It was just that standing in judgement in some other son's father's bedroom didn't hold the degree of terror that the path of my own father's wrath would have. The idea of a spanking just seemed ridiculous and silly compared to burning down the house. So it just came out that way.

He put me over his knee and I pretended that it hurt, because I didn't want him to feel worse than he already did.

The Day We Got TV
(Summer 1963)

We didn't have a television set in our house until I was almost ten-years-old. And we wouldn't have had one then, if not for an unexpected phone call.

"Quick! Run get your dad!" Mom got all excited. "He needs to come right now."

I found him in the backyard doing something with the flower bed. He was always doing stuff like that.

"You have to call KPOJ." Mom announced. "Right now. Here's the number. I wrote it down."

"What are you talking about?" Dad was as confused as I was.

"That was Frank on the phone," she could barely get it out. (Frank was Mr. Dixon, one of the teachers at my dad's school). "Frank said they just broadcast your name on the radio. They picked your name out of the phone book. You have fifteen minutes to call in. Here's the number. I'll dial it for you."

Dad looked at me and I looked at him and Mom danced around the room like it was Christmas.

But it was better than Christmas. It turned out to be real.

A few days later, Dad picked it up from the radio station and put it on a tray in our front room and we had a TV. It was black-and-white with a 13-inch screen and it was made of plastic, but it became the portal to a whole new Universe.

I never wanted to leave the living room after we got that TV.

Right away, my favorite program became the daily syndicated re-runs of *Leave it to Beaver.* Because obviously, me and the Beaver were just alike.

I immediately recognized that just like the Beaver, my life centered almost entirely around how to get through each day without getting into trouble.

I figured I could learn a lot about life from the Beaver.

I watched every day.

At first, I thought I wanted to grow up to be just like Wally.

Wally was so respected and everybody liked him and he seemed to know so much more than the Beaver did.

I think that's what my mom wanted too – for me to grow up to be like Wally.

But the more I watched the TV, the more I realized that it was Eddie Haskell who was having all the fun.

It Was Still Morning on the West Coast
(November 1963)

The loudspeaker startled us. Blaring something about teachers going to the office. Miss Bellow left the room.

In all my years, no teacher had ever left us alone in the room before.

It got quiet.

We just sat and looked at each other for a long time. A really long time. Eventually, Bobby Lee got up from his desk and went over to the window. Everything looked normal outside. Some kids started whispering. I didn't like it.

After a much longer period of not knowing and waiting, Miss Bellow came back to the class. She said:

"Sometimes things happen that don't make sense..."

And then she started not making sense.

She talked for a long time about something, but we couldn't figure out what it was, and she went on and on and on and she was rambling and I tried, but I couldn't follow whatever she was going on and on about.

That's when she started crying.

She turned her face away from us, moved over to her desk, sat down, put her head in her hands, and began sobbing.

Then we really got quiet.

Miss Bellow finally blew her nose, wiped her eyes, looked up over her glasses and said, "Soon, some of you will go home for lunch and find out that the President has been shot."

I was one of the kids that went home for lunch. I ran as fast as I could. Kennedy was dead. I knew who Kennedy was. Dad talked about him every night at dinner. Kennedy and the Democrats and the Socialists were destroying the Country. Dad always said Kennedy was the worst President and that it was Kennedy's fault about the Bay of Pigs. That's how I found out that pigs could swim. I had never seen pigs swimming, but I imagined that it might be a pretty neat thing to see, if I ever got to see it, especially if there were a lot of pigs swimming at the same time, like in a bay. So I thought maybe now I might get to see it, and anyway now with Kennedy gone, we could get rid of the Democrats and Socialists that were ruining the Government and the Country could finally get back on track.

When I got home, Mom already knew about Kennedy.

But she was crying too.

What?

I was sure Dad would take a bigger view about the whole thing, but when he got home a few minutes later, he was just as upset as she was.

It was very confusing, and on the west coast, it was still morning.

Sunday, February 9, 1964

The day I turned 10 years, 4 months, and 21 days old, The Beatles appeared on The Ed Sullivan Show.

I remember standing alone in the living room, after the program was over, before I went to bed that night, gazing out through the big picture window that faced SE 48th Avenue.

I couldn't get over how much bigger and more interesting the planet had become. It was suddenly filled with so much more magic, wonder, and promise than I ever could have previously imagined.

What a world!

There were Beatles in it!

It wasn't that they were going to change the world.

They already had.

Monday, February 10, 1964

At breakfast, I asked my dad for a guitar.

He said: "No!"

Piano lessons: "Yes." Violin lessons: "Yes." Trombone lessons: "Yes." Rock and Roll? "Absolutely not! Never!"

So I got a job.

That very day.

Every morning before school, I rolled up bundles of The Oregonian, crammed them into the basket of my Schwinn 10-speed, and delivered them covered in ink and sweat to the list of people in the neighborhood willing to pay a kid $2.25-a-month for the local news, ads and coupons.

It should have taken many months of saving and sacrifice to get that guitar, but incredibly, I did something that, to this day I still can't believe the-ten-year-old-me actually pulled off. I talked a friend (an older man at church who was in the music business) into selling me – on credit – a Lyle guitar that looked just like George Harrison's Gretsch.

I don't know why he did it.

I kind of suspected he might have been a pervert.

It was worth the risk.

The One True Nugget
(Spring 1964)

I was still just learning to play guitar, blisters and all, when we started talking about forming our first group (that's what we called them in 1964).

Roger's dad said we could use his garage and Twinkie's parents agreed to buy him a drum set. We didn't have microphones, or a PA system, so we commandeered the mouthpieces off a couple old telephones and wired them into cables and plugged them into our guitar amps. It totally worked. (The distortion was horrendous, but we didn't care.)

The guys wanted me to play organ, because I'd had three years of piano lessons and I played piano and organ at church. Plus, Ronny's mom had an old Hammond she'd let us use, as long as we were careful hauling it around. (And besides, Ronny was way better at guitar than I was.)

I wanted to be in the group so bad that I agreed to become our organ player – at first.

But I got lucky.

We were so excited about the group, and talked about it so much to anyone who would listen, that long before we ever played a single show, we were taken under wing by an actual professional theatrical agent, who just happened to be a friend of Roger's dad.

When the agent learned I was slated to play organ, he took me aside, shook his head, and said:

"You don't want to play keyboards. You want to play guitar. You should stand up front and sing. Girls like guitar players. And singers."

It was the one and only nugget of real-life-advice I ever got from any adult that turned out to be true.

World Without Love
(Spring 1965)

"Mom! Mom! Mom!" I pushed open the big oak door and ran down the hall shouting and stomping my feet and making as much noise as I possibly could. "I passed the audition! I passed the audition! I cant believe it! I passed the audition!"

"I'm in here, honey," she called out.

"They said 'Yes!'" I found her in the laundry room. "This is the best news ever. I get to play at the assembly!"

"You do?" She was folding diapers. "What assembly is this?"

"The big one. The biggest one of all. The End-of-Year-and-Hello-Summer-Celebration. The best assembly of the whole year!" I jumped up and down.

"Wow, that is exciting news," she folded another diaper, "and you get to play? What are you going to play?"

"My guitar," I bubbled, "and I'm gonna sing, too ... and play my guitar. I have to pick the perfect song. And I'm gonna need a new outfit – real jeans this time – Levi's – and one of those cool Bleeding Madras shirts."

"What's wrong with the jeans you have?"

"Ah Mom, they're old. I need a new pair for the assembly."

"There's nothing wrong with your good jeans. They're almost brand new."

"But they're not cool, Mom. They're just not cool. Everybody wears Levi's. Can't I ple-ea-ease have Levi's? And they have to be 501s."

"You don't need to try to be 'cool.' I think you're plenty 'cool' all by yourself. You certainly don't '... *need* ...' Levi's."

"No Mom, I do. I'm not cool at all. All the other kids have real Levi's 501s with buttons in the front. You always buy my jeans at JC Penny; it's *re-ea-ally* embarrassing. C'mon Mom. I'll never be able to show my face again if I can't get a pair of Levi's 501s – just one pair – oh, and a Bleeding Madras shirt."

"What on earth is a Bleeding Madras shirt?" She stopped folding for a second.

"It's the best shirt ever. It's all sorts of colors, kind of like plaid, but not really. Actually not-at-all like plaid. It has short sleeves or they could be long sleeves I guess but it has different colored lines and stripes going up and down and across and squares and its got a fairy-hook in the back. And it's just the coolest shirt ever. It would look so good at the assembly. C'mon Mom! This is my very first time ever – ever – to play and sing in public. This is really important."

"You sing at Church all the time."

"Church doesn't count. C'mon Mom. This is really important."

"It's '... *really* ...' important, is it?" She was wearing down. "When is this big, important concert?"

"It's not a concert Mom, it's an assembly and it's for the whole school. It's next week. We gotta go shopping. We gotta go shopping tomorrow."

"So you '... *have to have* ...' What? Not just Levi's, but Levi's 501s and a Bleeding Madras shirt, do you?"

"Yes!" I could feel her giving in. "And with a fairy-hook in the back. The shirt has to have a fairy-hook."

"What's a 'fairy-hook?'"

"Ah, You know, Mom," I had no idea how to explain it. "It's that tag-thing on the back of the shirt, near the top, right in the middle of the back. It's just a thin strip, like a hook. Made of the same stuff as the shirt. Sometimes people try to tear the fairy-hook off your shirt when you're not looking. But we have to make sure its got a fairy-hook. It's not cool if it doesn't have a fairy-hook."

"What? Why do they tear it off?"

"They just do. It's like a game the kids play, sometimes. Kind of like a joke. It's cool to have a fairy-hook and it's even cooler to get someone else's fairy hook off their shirt. I don't know."

"Why is it called a 'fairy-hook?'"

"I don't know, Mom. That's just what it's called." It's hard to explain these things to somebody who doesn't get it.

"Do you use the hook to hang the shirt with?" She was getting way off-track.

"No Mom, don't be silly, it's just for looks."

"Looks and hooks and Levi's and ... what is it ...? Bleeding Madras ...? Well, we'll have to see ..."

I knew she was giving in.

But I hadn't quite won. Not yet. So I went for it. "It's gonna be so great, Mom," I pretended we had a deal. "Now, I just gotta pick the perfect song."

I had to be careful. I needed her to feel like she was part of the decision, so she wouldn't change her mind about the shirt and the Levi's.

"You should sing *Moon River*," she suggested, "you sing that so well."

"Ah Mom, no. *Moon River* is fuddy-duddy," I protested, "I need something mod – or fab – or gear – something cool like The Beatles or The Dave Clark 5."

"What about *Hello Dolly*?" She started singing: "Hello Dolly, well Hello, Dolly, it's so nice to ..."

"No Mom," I stopped her, "this is serious. I need to pick the coolest song, ever."

"*Hello Dolly*'s not '... the coolest song, ever?'" She pretended shock and horror.

Now she was teasing me. That was a good sign. It was beginning to appear that maybe I was – just possibly – going to get everything I wanted.

"Prob'ly a Beatles song," I risked it, knowing she was not a fan.

"Oh honey, not The Beatles. They're just a fad. They can make any noise 'yeah, yeah, yeah,' and you kids are all so crazy about them that any goofy nonsense they put on a record goes straight to number one."

"That's because The Beatles are the best." I started it, so now I had to go with it. "They are great song-writers."

"Ha," she scoffed, "they're not song-writers. They're just popular, that's all."

"No Mom, that's not all. They're song-writers. And they're great. They write great songs." My logic was impeccable.

I knew I could win this argument, because I knew something she didn't.

"In fact, you know what?" I reeled her in. "John and Paul wrote a song and just to prove how good it was, they didn't even put their name – The Beatles – on it. They gave it to Paul's girlfriend's brother to record, so nobody would know it was them. And guess what, Mom? Guess?"

"What?" I had her.

"It went straight to Number One."

"Oh it did not." She was skeptical.

"Yes it did! It's called *World Without Love*. It's on the radio all the time."

"They didn't write that song." She didn't believe it. "That's Peter and somebody."

"Yes, yes! They did. It's Peter and Gordon. And Peter is Paul's girlfriend's brother. I have the record. It says 'Lennon/McCartney' right on it. I can go get it right now to ... WAIT! That's it! That's the song. That's what I'll sing. Oh Mom, you're the best. I love you sooooo much. Thank-you. That's the song I'm going to sing at the assembly."

She bought it.

Of course, I had to learn the chords, which proved to be much harder than I imagined, but it was such a cool song – (as well as the secret Lennon/McCartney composition that proved beyond any doubt that they were the greatest) – that I just kept at it, and at it, and at it, until I got it. And I did. I practiced it and memorized it and rehearsed it and learned it inside and out until I could play it in my sleep.

I was ready.

They called my name.

I walked out into the lights on that massive empty stage – just me and my guitar – in my Bleeding Madras Shirt and my button-fly Levi's 501s.

"Please, lock me away ..."

And there she was.

Linda Williams. The prettiest girl in school. Linda Williams turned and looked at me. Right at me. She watched me the whole time. I could barely breathe. I could barely think. I could barely feel my fingers. I didn't even know if I got the words or the chords right.

When it was over, she walked right up to me.

Linda Williams. The actual Linda Williams. The prettiest girl in the school. (I had drawn her name for Christmas presents in second-grade and I bought her a tiny glass carousel with three glass horses and I tied it up with a pink ribbon in a white box and I don't think she ever knew it was me). But magic. This was magic. This was it. My moment. Here she was. Linda Williams. She had noticed me. She was coming toward me. Not past me. Or anywhere else. To me. Right up to me. I watched her float towards me.

"You didn't wash your shirt," she shook the prettiest head in the school.

"What?"

"Your shirt – you're supposed to wash it," she smiled.

Linda Williams. Smiled. At me.

"It's brand new." I was nervous.

"Obviously it's brand new," she was being nice to me, "that's why you're supposed to wash it, so the colors will run together."

"Run together? I don't ..." I felt like I was blowing it.

"It's guaranteed to bleed," she explained.

"It's what?"

"Guaranteed to bleed," she repeated, "look, it says so right here on the tag."

She reached up. Linda Williams reached up. She put her arms almost around my neck. She leaned in toward me. Her hair smelled like Heaven. Her perfect skin came within an inch of my face. I held my breath.

"Yes. See?" She quickly gave my collar a jerk and yanked it toward my left ear. "It's right here on the tag. It says: 'Guaranteed to Bleed.' You're supposed to wash it in warm water so the colors all run together. That's what makes it look so groovy."

"Oh, ... groovy, ... thanks," I stammered. (I needed to pull it together. I had tried so hard to be cool. I felt all my cool slipping away.)

But it wasn't too late. I had managed to get the attention of the one-and-only Linda Williams.

"Just stick with me," Linda carefully patted my collar back in place. Then, with her magical hands, she gently smoothed out the shoulders of my soon-to-be-Bleeding Madras shirt and made me a promise, "just stick with me. I'll look out for you."

I gathered my courage and managed a smile of my own. "That's everything I ever wanted." I actually said it.

"You'll never get everything you want," she laughed, then turned, "but stick with me; you'll be alright."

"Is that a promise?" I didn't want her to walk away. I would have said anything to keep her there.

"If you're lucky, it is." She tilted her pretty head.

I desperately wanted to prolong our moment of magic. "So, what do I need? I mean, what do I need for the shirt, I mean, ... you know?"

"You already have everything you need," she assured me, "just wash it, you'll be fine. It's guaranteed."

I wondered if anyone so lovely could ever keep her promises.

"Guaranteed?" I asked.

"'Guaranteed to Bleed,'" she clarified as she walked away with my fairy-hook hidden in hand.

The Magic Ticket – Episode One
(Summer 1965)

I couldn't believe it was real.

When she handed it to me, all the air left my body.

It took me several seconds to figure out what was happening.

When all that air finally came rushing back in, I almost jumped up on her kitchen counter and started dancing around. But I was afraid she might not let me keep it if I did that, so I just danced up-and-down in place, waving the ticket wildly over my head.

As soon as I could manage it, I leapt up, threw my arms around her neck and gave her the warmest, most meaningful, most thankful, most sincerest, most heart-felt hug in the entire history of hugs.

Then I steadied myself and readied my eyes and carefully inspected every detail of that incredibly wonderful magical ticket again and again and again.

"August 22nd, 1965, Portland Memorial Coliseum, Section 208, Row A, Seat 3, Entry TT, Main Floor, $6.00, In Concert, The Beatles."

Un! Be! Liev! Able!

Toby Fuller's Mother bought me a Beatles ticket.

Me.

The Beatles.

I didn't know what to say. I didn't know what to do. I didn't even know she liked me. I had always only said, "Hello, Mrs. Fuller," to be polite whenever I came over and then I always went straight down to Toby's room. Toby's room was where I learned to play guitar.

Toby Fuller showed me my first chord. He explained to me which three chords went together. He taught me the names of each string and which notes were on which frets. Toby Fuller taught me how to tune my guitar and how to keep playing even when the blisters on my fingers started to bleed.

And now his mother had bought me a Beatles ticket.

When I got home, I was so giddy with excitement that I was absolutely blind-sided by the reaction, which in hindsight, I should have known was coming.

"You'll have to give it back."

"What? No! Wait? What? No! Why?"

"First of all, it's The Beatles. They're just a fad. Secondly, you're too young to being going to any concerts – especially Rock 'n' Roll concerts. But most importantly, and this is final, August 22nd is a Sunday. I don't know what the Fullers do on Sunday in their house, but as for us and our family, in this house, we remember the Sabbath day and keep it Holy."

All the air left my body again.

But this time, it didn't return.

It was over.

I could have argued that The Beatles were more than just a fad. And I could have pleaded that my tender age shouldn't disqualify me from experiencing such an important historical event. But I didn't even try, because I knew I was never going to get around that third thing – the Sabbath thing.

Numb, I knocked on Mrs. Fuller's door. She answered. I tried to hand her back the ticket. She wouldn't take it. I explained about the Sabbath. She still wouldn't take it. She offered to talk to my parents. I told her it wouldn't do any good. She was sorry. It was her turn to gave me a hug. She told me to keep the ticket anyway, to put it away, to save it, and to not tell my parents.

I didn't tell them. I saved it. I put it in my treasure chest with my Baby Book and my school pictures and my birthday cards and my Certificate of Baptism.

Toby Fuller told me that the concert was the best thing that ever happened to him in his whole life and that someday my unused ticket would probably be worth a lot of money. He told me to keep the ticket in what he called "...mint condition." He explained I should put it in plastic, keep it pressed flat and away from the air, and to be super careful with it.

I did everything he said. I kept it stashed secretly away.

Through the years, I dug through my treasure chest from time to time to make sure it was still there, but I never actually touched that ticket again. I only looked at it through my deep disappointment and its protective plastic covering.

ShitButtAssBiteHellFuck!
(Spring 1966)

It was our secret password.

"ShitButtAssBiteHellFuck!"

It was our salutation.

"ShitButtAssBiteHellFuck!"

It was almost the name of our first band.

Well okay, "… almost the band name" is a bit of a stretch; we did discuss it, but we knew we were never going to say it out loud in front of any adults.

And that was the magic of ShitButtAssBiteHellFuck – it was just for us.

It was something adults and squares had no access to. It seems juvenile and stupid now, of course, but for a bunch of pre-teen, mostly-Mormon boys starting a rock group in Oregon in the mid-sixties, it was edgy, even dangerous.

And we used it every chance we got – when we greeted each other – when we counted off a song at band practice – when we slammed the car door after being dropped off at church – when we walked out of any room with any adult authority figure in it – "ShitButtAssBiteHellFuck!"

We'd say it real fast, or just under our breath (or shout it out loud when there was nobody else around). A big part of the fun, of course, was constantly testing how close we could come to getting caught.

And we got braver with practice. It wasn't long before we could almost go wild with it, because as it turned out, the adults around us had no idea what was going on.

I first noticed the extent of collective cluelessness of grown-ups right after our very first gig.

It was Sherry Lisonbee's birthday party. We set up our amps in the basement where Sherry's mother had hung streamers and replaced the regular light bulbs with black lights for atmosphere - which was nice.

But the really nice – really big – uber cool – thing that Sherry's mother did for us was that she made all of the adults go upstairs when the party started.

When Twinkie's mother (Twinkie was our drummer) picked us up after the party, we threw his drums, along with our amps and guitars, in the back of her station wagon and all piled together into the back seat, still giddy and excited.

"How was the party?" Twinkie's mother backed out of the driveway.

"Fun," I volunteered.

We all grinned at each other.

"How did you boys do?" She asked.

"Well let's see," Roger took over, "first we played every song we knew, then we made out with the girls in the dark until Sherry's mom turned the lights back on."

"Oh, you boys are so funny," Twinkie's mom laughed.

I quickly reached over the seat and turned the car radio up loud, pretending I wanted to hear the song that was playing. I glared at Roger. I gave him my best look. So did Twinkie. Roger was the only non-Mormon in the band, so maybe he didn't fully understand how much trouble he could have got us into.

Using only our eyes, with no words at all, Twinkie and I together told Roger, in no uncertain terms, to keep his big mouth shut. Because what had really happened at the party was that we had played every song we knew and then made out with the girls in the dark until Sherry's mom turned the lights on.

Roger grinned back at us. He understood just fine. He just liked to flirt with getting us in trouble.

I watched Twinkie's mom very closely, as she drove, for any telltale sign that she had caught on to Roger's daring stunt.

She hadn't.

She didn't show any sign at all. She was just driving and humming along with the song on the radio. It was obvious to me that she didn't really know the song, though. She was just pretending, so we would think she was young and cool. But she wasn't young and cool. She was old and clueless.

I told myself right then and there that I was never, ever going to grow up to be one of those clueless old grownup fools. ShitButtAssBiteHellFuck!

Amerika

(March 1967)

It was the longest, smelliest, most uncomfortable Greyhound Bus ride in the history of long, smelly bus rides. It was hundreds of miles further, and a-day-and-a-half-longer, than we had counted on. I was convinced the torture would never end.

We sat in the very back of the bus, right next to the shitter. The odor was repulsively sickening, but we couldn't move, because we were hiding out and didn't want to attract attention to ourselves.

The whole thing was Roger's idea. He was always going to get me in trouble. This was likely just the first of many misadventures destined to land me in hot water. I knew that. But he was my best friend. And he taught me lots of great stuff.

Seriously – lots of great stuff.

"Keep the lie as close to the truth as possible," he instructed, "that way it's more believable and easier to remember." So I told my parents we were going to Disneyland (true), because Roger had won a trip selling subscriptions (Not true, but that's where we got the idea) and that Roger's father was going along as a chaperone (totally false). Roger told his dad the same story, but the other way around, and incredibly, nobody checked. I swear, my parents were more naive than I was.

"What if my parents call your dad?" I worried.

"They can't. He's on duty all week and only has his radio," Roger reassured me.

"What if your dad calls my parents?"

"He won't." Roger seemed sure and he was much stronger than I was, so I went along, even though I was pretty darn sure we'd get caught.

That bus ride was, by far, the worst travel experience of my life. We were completely unprepared, underpacked, underdressed, and underage. I spent most of the trip playing out various getting-caught scenarios in my mind. But after what seemed like sixty-or-so-stops in every small town on the West Coast, the stinky old bus finally arrived in downtown Los Angeles.

That's when Roger showed me how to hitch-hike. An old man, whose stench was almost as bad as the shitter in the back of the bus, picked us up. He was really friendly though, in spite of the smell, and he gave us a ride all the way to the Disneyland Grand Hotel. We arrived mid-afternoon and approached the front desk.

They turned us away.

We hadn't thought that part through.

As we walked back out through the fantastically fanciful lobby, Roger shouted long and loud:

"Fifty? Bucks?"

He shouted it just as if it had been our righteous decision to leave the hotel in protest over the high prices, like fifty-dollars was the most unthinkably outrageous price on the planet (and actually, to us, it was).

"I know, that's ridiculous, isn't it?" A man approached us as soon as we got outside.

"I never heard of a hotel costing fifty-dollars," Roger pretended the price was the problem.

"Hey boys, I've got an idea," the man proposed, "I have a friend, and there's two of you, so that's four, and there's two big beds in each room, so why don't we all just bunk up and that's only $12.50 each. How long you staying?"

"Four days." Roger was doing the math in his head.

"But I," I interjected, "I don't think they'll let us stay here. We're not eighteen."

"Hell, you're not sixteen," the man grinned, "let me take care of that, I'll do the checking in. How much money you got?"

"We only have .."

Roger stopped me. "Enough," was all he would volunteer.

When we got up to the room, the man made a very big deal out of wanting us to learn his name – John – he even wrote it down carefully on a piece of paper and handed it to us, so we could learn it. It was very, very important to him that we call him John. That was my first hint that something might be amiss.

The second sign happened just before bedtime. John's friend – Jim – showed up. Jim seemed nervous. John introduced us all and then announced that we'd better put our travel-weary bodies to bed, because we were going to have a "… big day tomorrow at Disneyland."

Roger and I hurriedly stripped down to our underwear, and quickly scooted under the covers together in the bed closest to the window, but John and Jim went into the bathroom, closed the door, and had an argument.

Roger and I stared at each other and tried hard to listen to what they were arguing about. We couldn't make out many of the words, because the TV was on, and we were afraid to get out of bed to turn it down. But clearly, there was some major dispute, because they argued a long, long time.

In the morning, Jim was mysteriously gone, never to return, but John was still right there, awake and ready for us. He had already brought up a pile of pastries from the lobby along with a large pitcher of orange juice.

We were so excited to get to Disneyland that we gulped down our free breakfast, got dressed as fast as we could, hurried across the parking lot and then had to wait for nearly an hour before we could buy our tickets and get into the Park.

We had a great day. We rode the Matterhorn. We explored Tom Sawyer's Island. We ate chocolate-covered-bananas. We met two girls. Roger disappeared somewhere with one of them and I kissed the other one in that ride where you go inside the microscope. We went through three times in-a-row. It was really fun.

When we got back to the hotel, John was there waiting for us. He had a stack of photographs he wanted to show us. It was important to him that we look at them. They were all candid photos he had taken in public places (many at Disneyland) of people's torsos. Only torsos. Male and female. Not faces. Just bodies. Not even legs. Just chests and bellies and backs and butts.

I finally, officially, but quietly, completely freaked out.

As soon as it was almost polite to do so, I handed the stack of photographs back to John, not knowing what to say, and hastily retreated right out of the room – out onto the balcony. I called for Roger to come out too. I immediately started to whisper, asking Roger what we were going to do to get away from this guy. Before we could formulate a plan though, John followed us out onto the balcony. He pulled up a metal chair and sat down next to Roger.

John began peppering Roger with all sorts of questions. Roger didn't seem perturbed or anything, but he never looked at John in the face. Roger just looked away – out into empty space – like he was unaffected, as he blandly answered each of John's questions.

John was so focused on Roger that I was free to sit back and observe and witness the deadly game unfold. And I saw something. Something I hadn't ever noticed before. Roger was strong. He was resolute. I always knew he was physically strong – maybe the strongest kid in school – but this was another kind of strong altogether. Roger was inside-strong. He was not afraid.

John began gently, slowly, nastily stroking Roger's arm. Roger allowed it. Roger didn't move a muscle. But it wasn't weakness. Roger wasn't frozen in fear, like I would have been. Roger simply sat and endured the creepy touching.

It wasn't panic that held Roger still, though; it was strength.

It was strategy.

John must have sensed it. Roger was not ready to be taken advantage of. So it was John's turn to retreat. He left the hotel room and didn't come back for a long time.

When he did return, Roger and I were already tucked under the covers in our bed. Roger was laying closest to the door, with his back to it, facing me. I was laying furthest from the door, but facing both the door and Roger.

"He's coming in," I whispered.

Roger braced himself.

"He went into the bathroom," I quietly reported.

"He's not coming out."

"Why is he in there so long?"

"What's he doing in there?"

"Wait! Shhhhhh! Here he comes."

John walked gingerly over to our bed and sat down on the edge next to Roger.

Roger turned onto his back and glared up at the ceiling. Ready.

John reached up. He pulled down the covers from Roger's shoulders and said: "Listen boys, as long as we're here, we might as well enjoy ourselves."

"You touch me and I'll fuckin' kill ya." Roger said it calm and steady.

And he meant it. He would have killed him.

I believed it.

And so did John.

After a few motionless seconds with nobody breathing, John slowly, carefully, replaced the covers up over Roger's shoulders. John stood up, went over to his own bed and slid under his own set of blankets.

The next morning, Roger retrieved the knives from under our pillows, placed them unobtrusively back on the room-service tray, and called his hippie aunt in Tarzana, to come pick us up. She did. She took us to Hollywood and showed us all the freaks with their wild hairdos and strange clothes. She let us stay at her bungalow the next two nights, and even set us up on dates with a couple of girls.

While Roger and his date rode the carousel on the pier at Santa Monica, I went for a walk on the beach with mine; she showed me how to French kiss. Roger's hippie aunt drove us to the bus station when it was all over. We suffered the long ride home and made it back to Portland exactly on time and neither Roger's dad, nor my parents were ever any the wiser.

I told you I learned a lot from Roger Garber. He was my best friend.

How Many Roads?
(May 1967)

I started it.

"I think we should take *Blowin' in the Wind* off the setlist."

"But it's Bob Dylan," Ronny insisted.

"Dylan's cool and all," Roger agreed with me, "but it's just not Rock'n'Roll. It's not hard enough. Musically, it's got no edge."

"But we need every song we've got," Ronny wasn't ready to give in, "and we already know how to play it."

"I like Dylan as much as anybody," I was bolstered by Roger's support, "and I agree that it's a great song – it is – I get it – but the stupid folk-singing club is always singing *Blowin' in the Wind* every time you turn around. I mean, c'mon – they're FOLK SINGERS! They just suck all the cool right out of Dylan."

"What do you want me to do?" Ronny tried to reason with us. "I have to get the set list approved before the show. The deal was we have to have twenty-five songs. And we're gonna be short without it. We gotta keep it."

"Look guys," Roger figured it out, "leave it on the setlist for the Principal's approval, so it looks like we have enough, but then we don't have to actually do it at the show. We can stretch out *House of the Rising Sun* and *Louie Louie* if we need to fill the time."

"Okay, that makes sense. Leave it on the list," I compromised, "but we're not going to actually play it."

So Ronny wrote out the setlist and turned it in:

PROPOSED SETLIST
Milwaukie Jr. High Spring Dance - Friday, May 19, 1967

Steppin' Stone
Satisfaction
Paint It Black
Get Off My Cloud
Sunshine of Your Love
Turn Turn Turn
My Generation
Drive My Car
I Want To Hold Your Hand
I Should Have Known Better
No Reply
Nowhere Man
Please Please Me
All My Loving
She Loves You
Twist and Shout
Taxman
She's Not There
Wild Thing
House of the Rising Sun
Last Kiss
For Your Love
Blowin' in the Wind
You Really Got Me
Louie Louie

The Principal looked it over, scribbled on it, and handed it back to Ronny with *Blowin' in the Wind* crossed off.

"What's this bullshit?" Roger exploded when he saw it. "What the fuck is wrong with *Blowin in the Wind*?

"I don't know?" I confessed. "But we weren't going to play it

72

anyway, so it doesn't matter."

"That's not the fucking point." Roger was incensed. "I'm going to talk to that old bastard, right now. And you're coming with me."

"No Roger," I warned, "that's a mistake. Don't cause a stink. Don't make him mad. He won't let us play. He'll cancel the whole show. Don't say anything, please. Just get along. It's not that big a'deal."

"I just want to know why." Roger would not be deterred.

"It's unpatriotic," Principal Warrant asserted in response to Roger's petition.

"What? How is it unpatriotic?"

"I assume you are familiar with the lyrics?" He condescended.

I began politely reciting the lyrics to show him that we did in fact, know them: "How many roads must a man walk down, before ..."

"Not those lyrics," he interrupted.

"Which lyrics?" Roger challenged.

"Banning cannonballs, among other things."

"What's wrong with banning cannonballs?"

"I told you. It's insufficiently patriotic." Principal Warrant was not to be swayed. "I don't know if you boys realize it, but there's a war going on in Southeast Asia, and we're going to support our servicemen – period. I'm not having any of this peacenik propaganda worming its way into our school. It's simply subversive and we're not going to allow it."

"Subversive? But .." Roger stopped and looked silently through the other songs on the setlist.

"Like I always say boys," Principal Warrant summed up, "in life, you have to decide which road you're going to take. The high road? Or the low road? There's no middle road. Now, take it off your list or don't play the dance."

"No, no, no," I jumped in. "No problem sir, we'll take it off."

"I expect you to do the right thing." He dismissed us. "Have a good show, boys."

"We're playin' it," Roger determined as soon as we got out into the hallway.

"No, he'll kill us. We'll never get to play again," I was horrified. "Besides, you don't have to sing it – I do. I'm the one who'll get in trouble."

"Oh nonsense," Roger scoffed, "we'll all get in trouble. What's he gonna do? He can't kill us."

"He could suspend us," I calculated. "One thing's for sure: he'll never let us play at school again."

"Who the fuck cares? It's fucking-Milwaukie-fucking-JUNIOR-fucking-High-School. We gotta get better gigs, anyway." Roger was on a roll. "And you! You pussy! You're going to have to get over your candy-ass fear of getting in trouble all the time. You can't live your whole life afraid of every fucking Principal Warrant that comes along. Besides, when we play it – and we will – it'll be his own fault, anyway."

"How do you figure?" I asked.

"He told us to take the high road."

Roger was right.

We played it anyway.

Les Could Have Been More
(1967 - 1968)

I guess I never really knew Lester Godfree. There was a gulf between us. (He was a few years older than me, and when you're young, that makes a big difference.) But I liked Les and looked up to him. One day, my dad warned me that Les was "... troubled." So I sort-of-understood maybe why I felt such a connection with him.

But the close connection Lester felt with our family was clearly not because of me – it was because of my father. Like my father, Les was a gifted natural athlete. He played football and basketball and baseball and was always on the winning team. Les was famous in our town. The same way my dad had been famous in his town.

It wasn't unusual for the athletes my dad coached to hang around our house after school and on the weekends, but Les was special. He was around a whole lot more than any of the others. So much so, in fact, that we got used to him being at the dinner table.

I always liked it when he stayed.

But the first time Les came back from Vietnam, he was different.

And it wasn't just his haircut. There wasn't as much life behind his eyes as there had been before. He was still patient with me kind even – and he listened to the stories I couldn't wait to tell him. But there was even more distance between us than before. I could feel it.

I asked him if he'd killed anybody over there.

"Oh, yes," was all he said.

I asked what that was like, but he didn't answer.

Lester's job in Vietnam was to sit on the runner parts of a helicopter and shoot at Charlie in the jungle. The Army gave him some special armored tiles to place around him to protect him from enemy fire while he was exposed out there on the runners of the helicopter, but Les told me that he didn't use the plates – that he just stacked them up and sat on them.

"I don't want to get my ass shot off," was how he explained it.

The second time Les came back from Vietnam, I could tell that he only came by our house out of a sense of obligation, and little else. He wore his uniform and remained very rigid the entire duration of his short visit. I tried to ask him questions about Vietnam, but he didn't seem to hear me and he didn't stay very long.

I did ask him if he was going to play football at the University of Oregon when he got out of the Army, but he said he had volunteered for "... another tour of 'Nam."

Just before he got away, I followed him out to the driveway and managed to ask if he was still shooting at Charlie from the runner-parts of the helicopters.

"Yeah, it's what I do. I'm good at it."

He turned and walked down the driveway and never came back.

Confessions of a Serial Asshole
– Part One: Be Special
(February 1968)

I'm not thrilled about this chapter, but it would be dishonest to leave it out. So here goes ...

It was not my fault that I could run faster than everybody else. Seriously. It had nothing to do with me. It was an accident. I didn't ask for it, expect it, or do anything to deserve it.

It also had nothing whatsoever to do with all that nonsense that teachers, coaches, salesmen, gurus and motivational speakers always try to get you to buy.

It was simply serendipity and it was both the best, and the worst thing that ever happened to me. It was the best thing, because it garnered me tons of attention, which I embraced whole-heartedly, and it gave me boatloads (and I do mean boatloads) of self confidence. But it was also the worst thing, because it instilled in me the pernicious (and false) idea that being the best at something was integral to my value as a human being. I've struggled with that destructive infection ever since. Not at first, of course; when it first started happening, I honestly didn't know that it wasn't my fault. I thought it was because I was special.

I thought it was because I was better than everybody else.

(It wasn't until many years later, long after it was too late to take advantage of it, that I discovered the reason for my freakishness. In a biology lab at Arizona State University, when I was a grad student in my mid-30s, the lab exercise was to practice taking VO_2Max

measurements – maximal capacity to uptake, transport and utilize oxygen. My results were more than twice as high as the next highest measurement the lab had ever seen. We thought it was a mistake, a miscalculation, an equipment malfunction of some sort, so we tested it again, and again, and again. The professors couldn't believe it. I scored off the charts every time no matter how we adjusted for error. That's why I've never had a DUI. I can pass any breathalyzer test simply by breathing out the volume of a normal person with less than a quarter of a breath. It frustrates the bejesus out of cops. But that's a different set of stories, for a later time.)

I may have exploited my advantage differently had I known the nature of it when I was a youngster, but I didn't know. I just thought I was special.

Here's how it happened:

By freshman year, I didn't like going home from school. Home wasn't a pleasant place. My dad could always find something wrong. I couldn't count on being left alone in my room, or being allowed to go to Toby Fuller's house to play guitar. (Plus, my parents had worked it out with Twinkie's parents that our band practices were only allowed on Saturday – never on a school night.) So I was on the lookout for after-school activities that would keep me away from the house. But it was tricky; I couldn't pick something that happened just once a week, I needed something every day. The logical answer was after-school sports. My father would totally be on board with sports and instead of being expected home by 3:00, I could stretch it out to close to 6:00, Monday through Friday.

So I went out for football in the fall. They didn't cut anybody, so I made the team. But I wasn't good. I wasn't quick. Or strong. Or terribly motivated. My 126 pounds sat on the bench, usually in my humiliatingly white, scrimmage-free, unblemished-by-action uniform, while the better players wore proud uniforms with dirt and blood and grass stains and got in the game. I just assumed that was my lot in life. Left out of the real action. I got used to it. The only problem was that football season ended.

So I went out for basketball. I was even worse at that. I couldn't make the orange ball go through the orange hoop. I couldn't jump. I still wasn't very quick. Or coordinated. But I was already familiar with the bench, so everything worked out just fine.

All the other kids were better at sports than I was. Okay. I wasn't surprised or upset. That's just the way it was. I accepted it and internalized it. I was fine with it. What I dreamed about was becoming the next George Harrison, so being bad at sports didn't matter to me in the slightest. During our games, I sat at the far end of the bench and wondered what I'd do when basketball season was over.

I was planning on going out for baseball. That seemed like the logical next step, but an accident of the calendar changed my life – for the rest of my life..

When basketball ended, baseball didn't start for two weeks – two whole weeks – two entire weeks of going home at 3:00. I just couldn't do it.

So I went out for track instead, because it was starting up right away. I didn't have to go home even for a single day. As ridiculous as it may seem, that seriously is the one and only reason I ever set foot on a track.

The coaches tried several events to see where to put me. I wasn't quick enough for the sprints. I wasn't strong enough for the field events. They made me try the pole vault for a few days, but I was wildly uncoordinated. So they did what they always did with the skinny kids with no special skills; they sent me over to practice with the distance runners.

Now in those days, we had a famous kid at Milwaukie High School – Jerry Gold. He had won all of the foot races in grade-school and junior high and was part of an AAU cross-country team. Everybody expected big things from him. So I was instructed, along with a handful of other misfits, to just follow him around. We did. We went on runs through the neighborhoods. We played on the train trestles. We threw rocks in the Willamette River. We got away from the school grounds for hours at a time. It was great. No coaches watched us or demanded we do any boring drills. We were free to goof off as much as we wanted. This running thing was going to work out just fine. I wasn't trying to win, or run faster than anybody else, or anything of the sort. I didn't even think about that stuff. I had no expectation whatsoever that track would be any different from football or basketball.

I was wrong.

The first track meet was at Gresham. The wind was blowing. Hard. And it was cold. The first event was the Freshman Mile Run. A whole slew of kids – twenty-five or thirty of us – reported to the starting line and I was intimidated by all the other runners. I looked around and wondered what the hell I was doing there. They all looked so fast in their spikes and singlets and shorts. I was certain this would just be more of the same. But the starter told us to take our marks and fired his pistol, so I ran. I didn't know what I was doing. I just ran. And I kept on running. And without even trying, I ran faster than everybody else and set a new school record.

I felt really bad for Jerry Gold. He was supposed to win. And I liked him. He was my friend. I wasn't trying to be mean or anything, but that very first race, I ran the mile in 4:42 and set the Freshman Record for both the school and for the city. I was fourteen.

When it was time to run the half-mile, I won that too. And then I won the two-mile. And every other race after that for the entire season. I went undefeated and Jerry never got a single win and it was neither of our faults.

Now importantly, a second layer of serendipity also came into play at this point – another mere accident – this one of place and time. This was all happening in Oregon. And it was happening in the spring of 1968. Steve Prefontaine was just down the road, a junior in high school, two years older than me. He was busy setting national records and getting his picture on the cover of *Sports Illustrated*. Oregon was suddenly crazy about running. Track and Field meets were becoming as popular as football. And Portland, where I lived, was a much larger media market than Coos Bay, where Steve was setting records. So into this crazy, once-in-a-lifetime combination of place, time and abnormal biology, I – without understanding why or how – accidentally inserted myself.

I started getting a lot of attention. People immediately started talking about the Olympics. I was going to be the next Steve Prefontaine. I started getting my picture printed regularly in the local papers. In fact, I could read different versions of my exploits every week in multiple publications. I was still doing my paper route every morning, but now, before I delivered the inky things, I could thumb through to see what they were saying about me. I loved it.

I was no longer anonymous. I was important. Everybody knew who I was. Everybody treated me differently. Walking down the halls at school was so much more fun than it had ever been before. Girls noticed me. Teachers gave me the benefit of the doubt. My father was proud of me. My peers deferred to me. Reporters wanted to talk to me. What a difference a few races had made.

And it went to my head.

To say I got cocky would be far less than truthful. Winning races was so easy that I started playing head games with my competitors during the races. I would talk to them, usually during the second and third laps when they were starting to hurt, and ask them why they even bothered to put their shoes on. They couldn't answer, because they were out of breath. I would tell them precisely when and where I was going make my move and leave them behind. I believed I could just run away from them whenever I wanted to, and they had all read my press clippings, so they believed it too. It worked every time.

Lining up for a race became so much fun. I would look around at the other poor souls who were about to be humiliated by me and think to myself how pathetic they were. I was going to win. I knew it. They knew it.

God liked me better than he liked them.

That's what I believed.

God was on my side.

None of my competitors in Oregon were ever Mormons and I belonged to the one-and-only true church on the face of the earth.

So I just knew that God liked me better.

And it wasn't just on the track. I walked around 24/7 like I was special. My self confidence exploded. I could walk up to anyone. At any time. And say any thing. Meeting girls became easy. Getting what I wanted became easy.

Life became a celebration of me.

I was the first person in my class to earn his Letterman's Jacket. I was awarded "Most Outstanding Freshman" for my undefeated year, then "Most Valuable" on the Varsity Team the next year. And on and on and on.

My future was bright.

And girls like guys with bright futures. They can't help it. It's in their DNA.

And I wasn't above taking advantage of that.

Girls and Guitars
(March 1968)

The day I started winning races, my father noticed. He started coming to every track meet. He evaluated each performance and gave me tips and reminders about race strategies – when and where to draft – when to surge – how not to get boxed in – and when and where to plan my kick. I paid attention, because my father had been State Champion in three events when he was in high school. (In fact, my dad's high school won the State Championship Trophy and he was the only one at his school that even qualified for the State Meet. Dad's three individual wins for 30 points were more than any other school in the entire state was able to garner.)

So my dad became my most important coach. He was the first one – the only one at the time, in fact – to pinpoint my exact advantage. He'd never heard of VO$_2$Max of course, but he quickly recognized what was happening.

"You can run farther than the fast guys and faster than the far guys." That's how he explained it.

"You don't have great natural quickness," he'd say, "so you're always going to have hold something back for a kick. And you'll never be a good long-distance runner; you're too tall and your mechanics are too pronounced to conserve energy over the longer distances. But right there in the middle, you can run hard and stay in high gear much longer than anyone I've ever seen."

So we focused on the mile and the half-mile. He dictated my diet and second-guessed my other coaches and tried to make sure I had no distractions that would keep me from performing at my best. My dad became my chief coach, strategist, and biggest booster.

He even started a new tradition. He'd take me out for steak dinners the nights before my competitions. Back then, he thought protein was the key and that meat was a good pre-race meal. I liked the steaks we would always order. But the much bigger deal about those nights was that my dad had never taken anybody in the family – ever – out to a restaurant before. And I got to go almost every week.

Dad's biggest concern – the topic that came up again and again at our steak dinners – was my motivation. He was very concerned that I was going to waste my gift, because I was far too easily distracted by the non-running things in my life – things that, according to him, I cared way too much about. Namely: girls and guitars.

So he took me to see Zig Ziglar. Zig Ziglar was a motivational speaker. Zig Ziglar had a big show at the Portland Memorial Coliseum (the same place where I didn't get to see The Beatles), and he spoke for about an hour-and-a-half and I don't remember much of it, but it was very motivational and it made everybody feel good.

I was sufficiently inspired by Zig Ziglar's speech that as soon as I got home, I did the one thing that I remembered him saying was the key to success.

Zig Ziglar said: "... Write down your goals."

In fact, I remember he added: "... And you students out there still in school, write down the five things you want to be true when you graduate."

So I did. I took my fourteen-year-old self up into my room and allowed myself to dream big for a few minutes. I fantasized wildly about my future. Mr. Ziglar said it didn't matter if it sounded crazy or fantastic or far-fetched, just to write it down anyway. So I tore a piece of paper out of my notebook and wrote down the five things that deep in my heart-of-hearts I wanted the very most to be true.

It was a crazy list. If I had shown it to anyone at the time – which I didn't – they would have never stopped laughing.

Before I graduate, I want to:

1) Go steady with the most popular girl in school

2) Be Student Body President

3) Own a Gibson Les Paul Gold Top guitar

4) Write a song and make a record and hear it on the radio

5) Be the lead guitarist in a big rock band and play a big rock show on a big rock stage in a big rock city where all the girls scream and clap and go crazy for me.

I could only write five things so there was no room on my list for anything about running.

I put my list in an envelope with an old birthday card and placed it carefully in my treasure chest next to my plastic-covered Beatles ticket and forgot all about it.

The Last Day I Danced
(Summer 1968)

I used to dance. Oh! Boy! Did I used to dance?

My entire body from my ears to my ankles was the end product of the analog audio signal path.

The spinning grooves in the vinyl records on the turntables in the studios of KISN Radio downtown would cause the needles of their equipment to vibrate and send signals out into the world as AM radio waves and the crystal receiver in my tiny plastic transistor radio would pick up those good vibrations and convert the electromagnetic radiation to sound waves that passed from my tiny three-inch speaker through my ears to my brain and my body would involuntarily erupt with unabashed motion, exuberance and joy.

I danced my ass off in my room.

And not only in my room. Out in public too. My whole body instantly transformed itself into music-made-physical whenever the groove got good to me. I loved that glorious feeling when your total being gives in to the sensations of song and you let yourself go.

I used to let go. A lot.

In the '60s, the Mormon Church held Saturday Night Dances. They'd be in different locations every week, but in the Portland area, there was one somewhere every Saturday night. And in those days, there was no such thing as a DJ (except on the radio). Every Saturday Night came with a live band. Which was awesome. As soon as I was old enough to be allowed to go, I never missed a dance. It was the best way to get close to girls. Sometimes, really close. And during the slow songs, dangerously close.

Then when my own band got to where we were good enough to get the gigs, we started playing the dances. It was a dream come true. Those dances were great opportunities for us to practice our chops, learn our craft and hone our performances. It was a great training ground that sadly doesn't exist for aspiring musicians anymore. But we were lucky. We had lots of chances to play and we benefitted from tons of opportunities to perform while we were still very young. We got to where we had a gig every Saturday night, at least. And when we added in the Friday night after-game dances during the sports seasons, we were busy.

The Mormon dances were usually held at Stake Centers, which are regional hubs with larger facilities than a regular church. Even modest Mormon church buildings are generally equipped with a full-size stage and an ample cultural hall, but these were even bigger and better. They all had great huge stages to play on – easily ten to twenty times larger than the accommodations in most bars and clubs and they often came complete with full lighting rigs and sound systems and backstage dressing rooms. We got spoiled, real fast.

And the Mormons danced. The dances were popular. The halls were always packed. Sometimes it took a few songs to get them started, but once they did get movin', it was all downhill. We were rock stars in training.

The only hurdle each night was how to get it all started. We experimented with different openings – changed up the song selections – and pretty quickly figured out which of our cover tunes were likely to make people jump up and start wiggling around.

Steppin' Stone worked well as a starter. *Good Lovin'* by the Rascals was also a motivator. But the sure-fire get-em-up winner was The Rolling Stones, *Satisfaction*.

So that's what we usually started with. I'd launch into that infectiously cool riff on my guitar – *Da-da, da-da-Da* – and by the time the band kicked in, we usually had the crowd on our side within the first few seconds.

Except one night. I remember it was at the Stake Center in Beaverton. I cranked up my amp and stomped on my fuzz-tone pedal and went into the lick and nobody moved.

Da-da, da-da-Da ...

All the girls were sitting way over on one side of the big empty hall in their hairdos and Saturday night dresses, while all the guys in their best clean outfits were all the way over on the other side. And the room was cavernous – three or four full size basketball courts at least. We were up there doin' our best rockin' and rollin' on stage. But it was a bunch of dead empty nothin' in the middle of the room. There were a hundred-or-so early arrivals still stuck to the walls nervously looking around and waiting for someone else to get it started.

I cranked it up a bit and played a little harder and started into the lyrics with as much animation as I could muster, trying to motivate some action:

I cant' get no ... Satisfaction
I can't get no ... Satisfaction

One lonely guy on the far side of the room started across the floor all by himself.

Cause I try and I try and I try and I try
I can't get no, (da, da, da ..) I can't get no

Everybody watched him walk right across the middle of the dance floor.

When I'm drivin' in my car
And that man comes on the radio

Every eye in the room followed his progress as he carefully made his way over to the girls' side of the hall.

He's tellin' me more and more
About some useless information

He selected one lucky candidate from the long line of walled-up girls waiting and watching. The entire room monitored his progress as he leaned over and said something to the winner.

Supposed to fire my imagination

She shook her head violently from side to side. Her bouncy curls wagged from side-to-side, but her arms remained folded and the rest of her stayed right where she was.

I can't get no, ... Oh no, no, no ...

Shot Down! Denied! Humiliated!

Hey hey hey, ... That's what I say

He stood there motionless for a second or two. Then slowly turned and started the long walk back across the middle of the room.

I can't get no ... Satisfaction

All by himself.

I can't get no ... Satisfaction

While everyone watched.

'Cause I try and I try and I try and I try

We kept playing our hearts out.

I can't get no, ... I can't get no

Until he made it all the way back over to his own side.

No, no, no ..

We played every verse and repeated the chorus three times and still nobody danced, so I called *Born to be Wild*, which we usually saved for the end of the night.

And that worked. Soon everybody was up. But I couldn't stop thinking about the poor lonely guy and his tortuous walk of shame. I tried to look around to see if he had recovered. I systematically searched through the throng of dancers to try to locate him. And I inadvertently noticed something.

Everybody looked silly.

Here they all were in their best Saturday-night-outfits. They had gone to great lengths to get their hair and their outfits just right and had probably spent many hours getting ready to go out. Each and every one of them was clearly trying to look their very best. And then when they got everything just right, when it came time to put all their preparations and plans into action, what did they do? They went out in public and made fools of themselves.

I watched them wiggling and writhing around. They'd squirm and twitch and jerk and shimmy and waggle. They'd stick their butts out and throw their elbows one way or another. And they'd bop their heads from side to side and make goofy faces. And twist around and flutter and flounder and jump and they'd work up a sticky sweat of deodorant and perfume and perspiration and the room got steamy and all their perfect hairdos wilted. In their writhing dampness, they just looked ridiculous.

I loved playing those dances, because I was above them all. I was on stage. I stood up front in the center of the stage. And they were a pathetic mess of wiggle-around.

I did not want to be one of them. I never wanted to be that unaware. The more I watched them wiggle, the more horrified I became. The aggregate mass of movement in the collection of churning bodies was something that, as a band, we thrived on, but the collective tumult had always masked a whole lot of individual silliness before. That night in Beaverton, I focused in, up close, on each individual participant and I no longer wanted to be one of them.

I wanted to be cool.

I wanted to be better than them.

I wanted to be above it all.

So I stopped dancing.

It may not be the worst mistake I ever made, but it's right up there.

And it's one that I sincerely regret.

The Metamorphosis
(October 1968)

I realize of course that it sounds oxymoronic, but it's downright commonplace for Mormon boys to be extraordinary. Overachievement is an important part of Mormon culture – especially for the young males. Forged in the fire of public speaking from a young age, we learn the art of persuasion through the appearance of politeness, trustworthiness and believability. Mormons are big on appearance.

We become skilled at how to put our best foot forward. We memorize scriptures. We sing in the choir. We put on shows. We force our bodies out of bed at ungodly hours to attend Seminary each morning. Compared to our non-Mormon counterparts, we learn not just discipline, but more importantly the vital importance of being able to distinguish ourselves from the mere mortals around us (humility is not necessarily encouraged).

Now in places like Utah (and parts of Idaho and Arizona) the thickness of all this extraordinariness becomes an insincere sticky syrup. But in Largely non-Mormon populations (in places like Portland), it's a genuine advantage. It makes it easy to stand out.

And I was no different. There's a reason I was always the front man of all my bands. I learned to sing in church. And not just to sing. I learned to force a twinkle in my eye. I practiced being the center of attention. I practiced charisma in front of the mirror. I learned how to publicly tell a story to the person in the back of the room. I practiced appearing to be like-able.

I also had the highly improbable good fortune of having some fantastic examples of extraordinariness to examine and emulate. The cohort just two years ahead of me in our tiny Portland 9th Ward (Mormon congregations are called Wards), harbored three genuinely incredible young men that, even by Mormon standards of special, were obviously destined to go out into the world and achieve greatness. Everybody recognized that they were unusual (and as it turned out, they actually were). I watched them intently and listened to them closely and learned from them more than they ever knew.

The first was Randy Boone. He was a musical genius. Besides being one of the kindest and most attentive humans on earth, he also had perfect pitch and a photographic memory. I could play for him any new song that I wrote – just me and my guitar – one time through. Randy would sit, arms folded, and listen to me with his back to the piano, without taking notes. When I finished, he could turn around and not only play my song, but he could write the whole thing out in musical notation, including the lyrics, and within minutes, I would walk away with a complete score of my new composition. He would even throw in extra arrangements - other parts that he thought would compliment the piece. And he was always right on. I never knew anybody else – ever – who could do that. The adult Randy Boone became the Director of Music at Disneyland for many years and finally the head of the Music Department at BYU.

My second role model was Greg Hanson. His gift was movie-star good looks, a magnetic personality, and razor-sharp radar for opportunity. He starred in every theatrical production, both at church and school and made it all look effortless and natural. He started a personal training business right after college that became hugely popular and he became a fore-runner of turning the fitness craze into the personal-growth craze. He was the pre-Tony-Robbins Tony Robbins and essentially invented the life-training-for-profit business model. I've been told that he parlayed his personal charisma into opulent mansions on both coasts.

But the smartest of them all – and the bravest – was Mikal Gilmore. (He became an editor at Rolling Stone.) He was the first boy in Portland to grow his hair out long – over his ears – even over his eyes. He challenged authority in a very dangerous way. His red hair flipped up in front as it grew longer and longer. He defiantly went around in public with a big "I'm not going to be what you expect me to be" sign right there on top of his head. And it wasn't just his hair. He was also the first person I ever saw pound on the pulpit with passion and righteous indignation during a Sunday night meeting at Church. (Mormons don't do that – we are generally expected to behave with conventional reverence – especially inside the chapel.)

But Mikal possessed a rare combination of intellectual, ethical, and political savvy. He delivered a powerful speech one night at Sacrament Meeting that I'll never forget, because he called us all out on our bullshit. Mikal pointed out that the word Jesus was in the name of our Church, but that we weren't followers of Jesus at all. Would Jesus be for the war in Vietnam and against the war on poverty? Mikal thought not. (Our congregation was overwhelmingly conservative and proud of being upstanding examples of Richard Nixon's silent majority.)

Mikal pointed out that instead of demonizing and railing against Communists and Socialists and Unions and Minorities, Jesus' message was to love – even our enemies. He challenged us to think about that.

Mikal's words were much more powerful, insightful and far more eloquent than I have either the memory or the talent to communicate here, but his exact words weren't what flipped the switch for me anyway. It was what happened next that did the trick.

Mikal finished his passionate plea for peace and love and sat down. Then the Bishop approached the pulpit and did something I never witnessed before, or since, in my entire life.

Incredibly, the following words came out of the Bishop's mouth: "I'd just like to remind the congregation that Mikal's words do not reflect the position of the Church on these matters."

Wow! Peace? Love? Not reflected? Not valued? Not subscribed to? Not part of the program?

That was the moment for me.

I didn't have Mikal's courage, so I remained silent and continued trying to put my best Mormon foot forward – for a while – because that's what was expected of me.

But that was the day I started growing my hair out.

I grew it out a little bit every day.

Confessions of a Serial Asshole
– Part Two: Be Shallow
(May 1969)

The tricky thing about learning from experience is that you can't always tell in advance which experiences are going to be the instructive ones. Some things, you may not even notice at all, when they happen. Sometimes they only affect you later. And sometimes the later ones hit you the hardest.

On May 31st 1969, Lester Godfree was killed in action at Per Fection, near Hamburger Hill, after having survived the 10-day assault to take Hill #937. The battle for the heavily fortified enemy encampment of dubious strategic importance that became the infamous Hamburger Hill ended on May 20th in a costly victory for the U.S. But the hill had already been abandoned by the Americans and reoccupied by the North Vietnamese eleven days later when Lester's helicopter was shot down near the Laotian border.

I didn't find out about Lester until later, though.

I wasn't thinking about Vietnam in May of 1969 – not in the daytime, anyway. I was thinking about Nancy Lattanzi and how her legs looked when she wore short shorts and about what kind of guitar I was going to buy when I got enough money and about how the shadow of my hair over my ears looked as I watched it float beneath me on the track as I ran my laps.

There were a great many problems in the world that May, but my biggest problem, according to my coaches – and my father – was that I didn't care enough. My coaches couldn't get me to work.

I never worked out on weekends or during breaks – ever. Not a lick. I told the coaches I ran, when they asked, but it was a lie. I didn't. I suppose they could tell.

Running and winning was so easy for me that I didn't think I needed to work at it. It was way more fun and interesting to spend my after-school hours and free time with Nancy Lattanzi, whose attentions I had magically commandeered, than it was go put on a jock strap and shorts and hurt myself running laps. I only went through the motions at track practice – I only did as much as I absolutely had to. I always left the track as soon as I'd done the bare minimum.

The coaches thought I was lazy. And I suppose I was. But the much bigger problem was that I just didn't care. I was so sure that I was special and that I'd always be able to outrun everybody that I didn't value my good fortune. Girls were paying attention to me and that was more than enough. Why would they ever stop?

When I didn't go undefeated my sophomore year, it wasn't that big of a deal. It wasn't as embarrassing as it might have been, because I had lots of excuses. I had stepped up to a much bigger stage and I was still only fifteen, so I got the benefit of the doubt from all corners. I could still outrun even the best seniors at most schools, but now, running Varsity, I had to compete against Steve Prefontaine and Mark Heifield and Doug Crooks and Carl Meininger and the rest of the crop of contenders for the crown – the handful of other Oregon high school milers with the potential to become world-class athletes and Olympians. It was a much bigger challenge than before and I wasn't all that interested in the necessary sacrifice.

As I said, I didn't do much training, but just by racing once-a-week, I did drop my mile time down to 4:20.1 (not bad for a fifteen-year-old), so as far as I could tell, nobody seemed to be losing faith in me, which was all that mattered. As long as people were still paying attention, that was all I cared about.

My lack of fire on the track was further de-fueled by Steve Prefontaine himself the last time I raced against him, when he was a senior and I was still a sophomore.

But just the opposite of the way one might think.

It was the State Championships on May 31, 1969 – the same exact day that Lester Godfree was killed in Vietnam – and it was Steve Prefontaine's last high school mile. I'd lost to Pre before, earlier in the year, but as I said, at my age, I wasn't expected to beat him, so there was very little pressure. What struck me about Pre in the staging tent before the race was that he seemed to care even less than I did. He seemed almost annoyed that he had to go through all the tedious steps of having to lace up his shoes and go out and actually line up and run the race. Now, I may have read him wrong (judging by the many other accounts I have read of him since), but my clear impression that day was that he was bored to death, and that he placed very little value on the contest that was about to unfold.

I was so struck by his demeanor that I said something to him about it.

"You're not nervous?" I asked him.

"About what?" He sneered.

"The State Championships," I insisted, "you don't look happy to be here"'"

Pre pointed to the thousands of fans in the grandstands and complained that their ugly faces were the only faces he was likely to see once the race started.

I decided to let him see mine.

The gun went off. I stayed with him for the first lap and a little bit more, but coming into the third turn, I knew I was in over my head. My lack of preparation jumped up and grabbed me. Hard. I faltered, faded and finally finished in 7th place, allowing far inferior runners to blast past me in the final stretch.

Many young athletes would have taken that as a lesson and re-doubled their efforts. Others might have taken it for a sign that they didn't really have what it takes and given up. Not me. I did neither. I took it as a sign that I was on the right track.

When we returned to the staging area, post-race, I was again seated next to Pre. He seemed exactly as thrilled with his win as I was with my loss, which is to say, there was no joy in it. Pre reached down into his dufflebag, pulled out a can of beer, popped the top, and took a swig. He didn't offer me one, but I wouldn't have accepted it anyway. We were surrounded by onlookers. I was sure he was going to get caught. I thought he was jeopardizing his win and his reputation. There were officials everywhere. In fact the Clerk of the Course – Dick Fosbury – the famous high jumper – was right there in the tent with us. But Pre didn't seem to care at all. I was amazed. The most-famous athlete in Oregon was actually drinking beer on the in-field at a High School Track meet – the State Championships no less – with thousands of people in the stands. He didn't appear to me to care whether he got caught or not.

It occurred to me that not caring was the key.

Not caring was cool.

Not caring certainly made losing easier to explain away. Not caring became my cushion against risking self-esteem. Not caring also made those messy problems out in the larger world like war and injustice much easier to cope with. And finally, not caring became an effective tool for setting yourself apart from everybody else, for bucking the trends, for not buying into the conventions, and thereby attracting attention – which is the one thing I did care about. I decided that he who cares least gets to redefine the rules. (which I later learned pretty much holds true for personal relationships, but is far less reliable in contests of athletic competition).

I began to practice and hone my own personal set of not-caring skills and I have to say that over the next few years, I became quite good at not caring.

The War was on TV
(June 1969)

When we got the news about Lester Godfree, I pulled the World Atlas down from my parents' bookcase to see how far it was to Canada.

I didn't know yet how I was going to get there, or what I was going to do when I got there, but I figured I'd better start making a plan.

I started watching the news.

The war was on TV every night.

Every night. In black and white. Boys. Lots of boys. Boys barely older than me. Every night. Blood. Bombs. Bandages. Bodybags. Flames. Mortars. Napalm. M-16s. Grenades. Explosions. Amputations. Stretchers. Mud. Fog. Smoke. Fighting. Pain. Suffering. Death. Every. Night.

I didn't want anything to do with it.

Was I was a coward?

I didn't know.

I was afraid. But it honestly didn't feel like cowardice – the kind to be ashamed of, anyway. The war just felt so wrong to me that fighting and dying for it just seemed stupid and pointless.

Besides, even if my feelings were just cowardice in disguise, no part of me had any desire to overcome, or get over it.

Hell, I didn't think overcoming cowardice was even an option.

It just made a lot more sense to me to run away and deal with the consequences later than to stay and fight and die.

It was a life and death decision.

Who can you trust with a decision like that?

I decided the smart move was to not tell anybody.

My Extraordinarily Successful Private One-on-One Interview with the Bishop
(June 1969)

"Have you been paying your tithing?"

"Yes." I was expecting the question and was ready for it.

"Have you been keeping the Word of Wisdom?"

"Yes." So far, so good.

"No cigarettes?"

"No."

"No alcohol?"

"No."

"Caffeine?"

"No."

"Do you masturbate?"

"What? No."

"Do you have wet dreams?"

"Huh? Well, I do have this one dream. I have it all the time."

"Tell me about it."

"It's always exactly the same. It's very scary. I dream I'm dead in the jungle. My body is laid out over a log and I am spiraling in the air looking down on my dead body. Sometimes I'm afraid to go to sleep at night, because the dream – the same dream – keeps happening, over and over again. I'm really scared."

"What do you think it means?"

"It means I'm going to die in Vietnam."

"You don't know what a wet dream is, do you?"

"No."

"Well, you don't have to worry about it. You won't die in Vietnam. We'll win the war long before 1968 is over. You won't have to go. Don't worry about it."

"You really think so?"

"I know so."

I never had that dream again – not even one time. I could breathe again. I felt so much better.

He was the Bishop.

He knew things.

(That's what I thought anyway.)

Of course, we didn't win the war in 1968. Or ever. But I didn't know that then. I only knew that the terrible dream went away.

It was comforting.

Mrs. Godfree's Face
(June 1969)

When David Summers came home from the war, his entire family gave talks Sunday night at church. David stood in his pressed uniform with medals and ribbons and confessed that he had fired his weapon blindly into a jungle of chaos and confusion and that he hadn't even seen any of the enemy he'd been credited with killing.

We were all hoping for a better story.

It wasn't David's speech, but the next one – his mom's – that changed everything for me. Not that she said anything unusual. She talked about how she had prayed for David every night and how God had answered her prayers and watched over David and how God had brought him safely home to the family that loved him.

From where I was sitting, as Mrs. Summers basked at the pulpit, I could see Mrs. Godfree seated quietly in the congregation.

Mrs. Godfree's son Les – only one year ahead of David in school – had also returned from the war.

Twice.

But not the third time.

I watched Mrs. Godfree's face as Mrs. Summers went on and on about thanking God.

I wondered what Mrs. Godfree was thinking. And feeling.

And I wondered why God hadn't watched over Les Godfree too.

The Road to the Heart
of Outer Darkness
(June 1969)

The cool thing about having a September birthday was that I got to start first-grade when I was five. I didn't have to wait another whole year to start growing up. Which at the time, I thought was great. All the other kids were older than me, but that was a plus; I learned from them. In fact, I always considered it to be an advantage – even a source of pride – to be the youngest in my class. It put me developmentally ahead of schedule in my imagination.

That all changed however, in dramatic fashion, my sophomore year in high school. That year, as the weeks rolled by, my classmates and peers, one-by-one, started turning sixteen, while I remained painfully on hold – at fifteen. That was a problem – a serious, year-long, frustrating, debilitating problem.

All that year, while my friends were having birthdays, getting licenses, driving cars and experiencing the precious autonomy and glorious freedom of being able to get up and go, I was stuck painfully in kid mode.

Still bicycle-bound.

Fifteen was an especially bitter year for me, because I was remaining fifteen in a very public way. I was the famous runner kid in school. People knew who I was. They were watching me. It was embarrassing to still be bicycle-bound. I was worried they'd look at me differently and consider me less important, less relevant, or tragically, somehow less cool. The vast chasm between my last birthday and the next one seemed interminable. And on top of all that, what made it even more painful and humiliating was my family's Mormonism. Mormons aren't allowed to date until they're sixteen. And my parents were sticklers.

Aaaaarrrrrrgggghhhh!

Even my Mormon friends were driving and dating. No amount of pleading, cajoling, or begging – no tantrum, no negotiation, no argument, no matter how reasoned and rational – was ever going to change my parents' minds. Rules were rules.

I somehow survived the shame and torture for more than eight whole months before I just couldn't take it anymore.

It wasn't like opportunities didn't exist. The logistics of a double-date could always be worked out. Cars had back seats. My non-Mormon friends didn't know – or care – that I'd be violating some arcane, arbitrary convention. So there was that.

And there was something else. Summer was coming. The sun was out. Jackets and sweaters were being put away. All the old coverings were coming off. New, fresh, lovely things were coming out. Life was happening. Temptation was everywhere.

And then the deal-breaker:

Patty Larsen. Patty was enchanting. Right now – not months from now. Desire doesn't have a pause button. Three-and-a-half months was forever. It was simply no longer possible to wait.

So I did it.

I asked.

She said, "Yes!"

Roger was taking Sarah. Roger would drive. Patty and I would have the back seat all to ourselves, both going to, and coming from, the concert.

We were going to see Steppenwolf.

"Yes!"

It was going to be great.

And it was.

Music, fun, love, peace, groovy, crazy, wild, young, dangerous, black lights, strobe lights, incense, crowds, sounds, smells, smoke, Magic Carpet Ride, Born to be Wild, … LIFE!

While it lasted.

I don't remember the lie I told my father to get out of the house that night, but it must have been weak, because by the time we dropped Patty off, it was after midnight.

And I knew I was caught.

I told Roger not even to pull into the driveway.

No reason to get him in trouble too.

"Just let me off on the corner and I'll walk to the house."

Sure enough. My father was waiting on the porch.

He was never going to understand. It wasn't in his chemistry. The recriminations, accusations, and character assassinations that followed were all expected. I endured them. You play? You pay! That's the deal. My only real concern was the exact nature of the specific consequence. What was the punishment going to be? That was all I needed to know.

And it came down hard.

I was grounded until my sixteenth birthday.

No privileges. No activities. No gigs. No band practice. No concerts. No shows. No dances. No parties. No outings. No trips to the store. No leaving the house for any reason, other than school and church (and then straight back home). Total lockdown until my sixteenth birthday – almost four long months away – the ENTIRE SUMMER OF 1969!

And there was no reprieve. There was never going to be a reprieve. My Father was never – ever – going to budge. And he didn't. I spent that summer scraping tile, sanding wood, and performing the assorted menial tasks I was given, as we remodeled the upstairs bathrooms in our new house on Oatfield Road.

While my peers were out basking in the sun and freely moving about the planet, going to movies and beaches and cookouts and fairs and festivals and celebrations and some of them even traveling across the country to attend Woodstock (yes, that summer), I was a prisoner of 16018 S.E. Oatfield Road, Oak Grove, Oregon 97222.

I imagined the worst of it would be that I'd be forced to quit the band. But Twinkie moved away that summer and Ronny got a job at a grocery store (where he still is today) and Roger promised we'd start up a new group as soon as I had served my sentence.

So I paid the price. I was willing to face the consequences. I did the time and, to be honest, to this day, I have never once endured a single twinge of regret. That night. That concert. That experience. That back seat. My magical time with Patty Larsen. It was all unforgettable.

But what I didn't expect – and didn't understand – was my mother's reaction the next morning.

Now, my mother is a wonderful human being. Ask anyone who knows her. I'm serious. Anyone. You will find no detractors. She is selfless and patient and loving and long-suffering. In fact, the very worst thing anyone can say about my mother is that she has always done what she believes is right. Yes, my mother is a saint. The problem, of course, is that she is also a Latter Day Saint.

She couldn't speak to me all that next day – and for many days after. I hadn't merely disappointed her, I had broken her heart. For quite a period of time, she couldn't deal with her pain.

She didn't speak to me. That surprised me. Not a single word came my way. The silent treatment. I felt like I didn't exist to her. I did hear her wailing during that first night and clearly heard her cry out: "I can't believe he came out of me."

She was afraid I was going to Hell. She was in so much anguish that she confided her fears to our Bishop, and he must have let it leak, because over time it became not-so-quietly understood in our community, and in our church especially, that I was a lost cause – on the road to perdition – headed for the heart of Outer Darkness – that's what Mormons call it – Outer Darkness.

That's the part I didn't expect.

I didn't like being grounded, but I understood it. I had broken a rule. There were consequences. Fine!

But I was astounded and bewildered that my transgression had both consigned my soul to Outer Darkness, and broken my mother's heart.

It just seemed to me to be unnecessarily cruel – all the way around.

The Castle
(Summer 1969)

Grounded and not allowed to leave the house for the entire summer of 1969, I was forced into a cocoon of social and psychological deprivation.   But by summer's end, I emerged transformed.

My transmogrification was accomplished by the serendipitous confluence of several key factors: a once-in-a-lifetime lucky accident of School-Distric-boundaries, the physical layout of our new house on Oatfield Road, and my very conscious decision to use the time to intentionally re-invent myself.

When my parents broke the news that our new house on Oatfield Road was just on the other side of the District line, and that I would have to change high schools for my junior and senior years, I was initially apoplectic. All my friends were at Milwaukie High School. I would have to start all over. It wasn't fair. And so on.

But once I saw the new house and my new room, and the more I thought about it, the more I realized that starting over, if I planned it just right, could be a very cool thing.   There were certainly possibilities.

I recognized that although my social status at Milwaukie High had soared once I began running and winning races, there was a limit to how far I could rise. Those kids knew me. They had known me since first-grade.   They remembered all my embarrassments and peccadilloes – every humiliation and failure since age five. Add to that, the fact that the social cliques at Milwaukie High were already firmly established. The country club set had recently allowed me access to their good graces, but I would never be a full-fledged member. I would always be nouveau popular – a late-comer – a climber.

At the old school, I would forever carry my past around with me. At the new school however, I could be completely unburdened. I could create a whole new persona and nobody would be the wiser. The kids at Putnam didn't know me – not really – they knew my name – my pictures were in the newspapers – but they didn't know my history. I could be anything I wanted to be. This was my chance.

To my great fortune, the physical layout of our new house on Oatfield Road also afforded further opportunities for transformation.

My new room had a large window that opened just above the roof of the garage. It was an easy, medium-sized step to get up and through that window and out onto the roof. There was a large old oak tree with thick sturdy branches right next to the garage and the biggest branch of all rose up over the roof and very nearly made contact with the gutters. It was nothing to get up and down that tree. I could do it easily without soiling even my best clothes. I was careful not to let anyone see me do it. I had to keep it a secret. (Over the coming course of literally hundreds of late night adventures, I never once got caught.)

But by far the most important aspect about that house on Oatfield Road was the girl next door.

My room was on the top floor and my window faced out so I had a view of the neighbor's back yard. They had a fence. And a pool. And a deck. And a sixteen-year-old bikini-clad California-beach-babe daughter that laid out on that deck everyday like clockwork. (It turned out she was actually Canadian, but from my window she looked like my favorite scene in every Hollywood beach movie.)

I couldn't believe my luck. I took my oversized Iron Butterfly poster and covered my window with it so my parents wouldn't catch on. I was sure that if they saw what I could see, they'd move my room to the basement and never let me back upstairs again.

Her name was Mila Winston. She had just turned sixteen. She was only a couple of months older than I was. Timmy Tucker gave me the scoop. (Timmy lived a few streets over and stopped by to introduce himself as one of my new teammates on the Putnam cross-country team.) I was immediately jealous that he knew more about her than I did. I still remember the way he initially described her:

"She's that girl that, when she walks into a room, it's embarrassing, because everybody has to try to pretend they're not looking at her. And everybody knows that everybody is pretending – it's that obvious."

"You mean all the guys, right?" I checked.

"No, pretty much everybody," Tim corrected me. "Guys, girls, adults, small children, fuzzy animals – pretty much everybody."

"You may be exaggerating a bit," I laughed, "I'm sure you get used to it after a while."

"Not really," Tim thought about it, "her name is Mila Winston, but everybody calls her 'Mila Winston – The World's Only Living Nine-Point-Nine.'"

"So, she's not a ten, then?" I ventured.

"It's widely recognized that there's no such thing as a perfect ten," Tim informed me.

"Hmmm, 'Mila Winston – The World's Only Living Nine-Point-Nine,' huh? So she's missing a tenth-of-a-point," I wondered. "What's her demerit?"

"We're still looking for it." Tim grinned.

According to Timmy Tucker, she was the most beautiful, smartest, sweetest, most amazing girl – ever. She was everybody's favorite. She got straight-As, volunteered for all the clubs, was nice to even the unpopular kids, and was elected both Rose Festival

Princess and Head Cheerleader when she was only a sophomore.

It appeared that the Mila Winston fan club was going to be a lot more crowded than I realized. I was more than a little disappointed to think that once school started, I would no longer have my beach babe all to myself.

But then Tim said something that got my attention.

"The definition of cool at Putnam High is whether or not you're friends with Mila Winston – The World's Only Living Nine-Point-Nine. You haven't really made it unless you're in her exclusive inner circle."

("Hmmm?" I thought to myself, "... and she's right next door.")

He continued. "Only then, do the lucky few, achieve the rank of 'coolest of the cool.'"

Ah! Ha! I had my mission.

Mila Winston – The World's Only Living Nine-Point-Nine – my next door neighbor – would be my ticket. I had to find a way to work myself into her circle. I needed to transition from peeping-tom to personal confidant. Did I dare dream it? Was it possible? I just had to work out how to pull it off.

Before I was able to formulate even the first sketch of a plan though, Tim saw my machinations at work and threw in one last obstacle. "Don't even try, Dude. She only dates college guys." Tim seemed wisely resigned to his fate as a lesser human being.

Not me. I was on a mission.

It turned out that it was actually only just one college guy that Mila was dating. I watched him coming and going from my window. He had a souped-up hot-rod Camero with a racing stripe, mag wheels and glass-packs. He made a lot of noise when he picked her up and dropped her off, so it was easy to keep track of them.

One late afternoon/early-evening before it got dark, just a few days after my introduction from Tim, I heard them coming. I quickly invented a reason to be in our driveway so I could get a closer look.

She got out of the passenger side, hopped around to his driver's-side-window and leaned in while they talked for a little while. As she stood next to his car with her elbows on the sill of his window, one knee bent flirtatiously, laughing like she didn't have a care in the world, I marveled at her long legs and her tiny butt and her thick flowing hair and tried to pretend not to be staring, just exactly as Tim had predicted. I laughed inside at how transparently I was embarrassing myself.

When the boyfriend finally backed out of her driveway and revved his engine and roared away, she started toward her front door, but as soon as the sound of his motor faded, Mila Winston – The World's Only Living Nine-Point-Nine – turned and came bounding across her front lawn in my direction.

"So you're the famous runner kid – eh?" She smiled, "I'm Mila."

I decided to play it cool and act all humble and self-deprecating, so I opened my mouth, ...

But nothing came out. Not even a stammer – nothing.

It was her skin.

Up close, her skin was like nothing I'd ever seen before. It seemed to have its own light source. She glowed. I'm serious. It took me almost an entire minute to recover. I very nearly blew it, but I collected my wits just in time and I responded:

"Yeah, ..."

"Well, it's nice to meet you," she covered for me.

(This is it. First impression. Get it together. Calm down.)

"We'll probably see lots of each other," she continued as if it was a promise, "being neighbors and all."

"I can see you from my window," I blurted.

(Why the hell did I say that? What's wrong with me? Holy! Shit! What an idiot!)

"I know," she smiled.

"You do?" I was horrified.

"Sure." She winked to let me know it was okay. "Why do you think I lay out on the deck everyday?"

She bounced back across the lawn with her hair following behind her and disappeared.

What the hell just happened?

Was that real?

Did I dream it?

I checked the world around me for any tell-tale sign of objective reality. The concrete in the driveway still had the same cracks as before. Wow! Was it true? Had I really managed to impress her by having my picture in the paper? And what? She wanted me to see on her on the deck? Oh! My! God! I didn't have to worry about the peeping-tom-thing. I had her permission? I couldn't believe it. Yes – I had her permission. And better yet – she knew who I was. And maybe – just maybe – I might have stumbled into the strange, wonderful, magical world of Mila Winston – The World's Only Living Nine-Point-Nine.

Over the days and weeks that followed I carefully cultivated and nurtured my exciting new friendship. Or more precisely, Mila did. She gave me little signs – sometimes just a glance, or a smile.

Sometimes she'd wave or flash a two-finger-peace-sign up at my window when she came out onto the deck. Sometimes, she would signal for me to sneak over and whenever I could get away, we would sit on her back steps and talk about the coming school year and about what we were going to do with our lives and about my upcoming races and about the rock band I was going to form and about her dates with Tom.

His name was Tom.

I do get points for being patient, for not over-stepping my bounds, and for playing it off like my only agenda was to be her next-door-neighbor-friend – 100% wholesome and innocent and above-board. I even managed to convince her that I didn't care about her dating Tom – like I could take it or leave it – like whatever happened was fine with me.

I knew (because she told me), that she hated it when all the boys fawned over her, so I never did. I made sure she didn't consider me just another one of her clamoring hopefuls. I played it off. I acted like ... yeah ... I liked her alright, but that I could live without her.

Sometimes when she would signal for me to come over, I couldn't get out from under my dad's watchful eye, so it wasn't possible to go. And that killed me – It really ate me up inside – because I wanted nothing more in the world than to spend time with her. But I kept that to myself and never apologized to her about not coming over. The next time I would see her, I would simply act like it never happened. If she asked, I'd pretend I didn't remember. I made her believe that while I did enjoy spending time with her, I'd be just as happy if we never spoke again. It was my best trick. And it seemed to be working.

That summer sure turned out to be a whole lot more exciting than I expected.

The best times were the late nights after everyone had gone to sleep. I could always get away then. She'd come home from a date, say goodnight to Tom in the driveway and pretend to go up to her room. But then she'd hesitate at the front door, glance back over her gorgeous left shoulder at my window and give me the sign to come over. I'd silently slide open my window, step out, scurry down, hurry over to her back steps and spend countless blissful hours basking in the wonder that was Mila Winston – The World's Only Living Nine-Point-Nine.

Our nightly rendezvous quickly became the most important part of my life. Nothing else mattered. And as the summer progressed, so did we. For a while, we found each other almost every night. And then it became *every* night. I came to depend on our time to be together. I continued to wait for her signal, because I was still playing it cool, but she always invited me over. Without fail. And it finally began to dawn on me that she liked our nights together, too.

But did she adore them the way I did? Did she? Did I dare hope for that? (Too late – I already hoped for that.) Did she like me too? The way I liked her? So much that it hurt? It was torture not knowing. I realized I was in a lot of trouble. I didn't know how long I could keep this up.

Then it happened. The very last night before school started. That last night of summer. Just as I was carefully laying out my first-day outfit. I heard the sound of his engine and the crack of his muffler. I went to the window. She didn't get out.

She didn't get out for a long time.

When she finally did exit his car, she went straight to her front door. Opened it. Did not look back over her gorgeous left shoulder. And stepped inside.

My heart fell.

I'd often wondered what I'd do if she didn't invite me over one night, but now it had happened. It was awful. It hurt. Bad. Real bad.

I didn't think I was going to be able to show up for the first day of school. I didn't know how I could possibly see her in public and not give-away the hurt I was feeling. How could I do that?

Then I saw the porch light. She turned it on. She was standing beneath it.

I didn't even bother with the tree. I jumped off the roof and ran to her. She looked like she might have been crying.

We went to our step.

I waited.

"I broke up with Tom." She finally said it.

I let go the biggest breath of my life.

I caught myself. I didn't want to appear joyous, because she was clearly upset. I promised myself I'd celebrate wildly as soon as I got back to my room. But I couldn't let on. I was so excited that it was a major struggle to keep my composure while I comforted her. But I'm a pretty good actor. We talked for a long time. She said it was her idea to break up. And that it was hard.

I was so understanding that I surprised myself.

She revealed more and more and more to me. And I let her. She finally confided that the deal-breaker was that Tom was continually pressuring her to go all the way. And that she didn't want to go all the way. Not yet. And that's how she knew it was over with him.

"That's not cool," I consoled her. "Nobody should pressure you into sex. Nobody should make you do anything you don't want to."

"That's just it," she confessed, "it's not that I don't want to. I do want to. I *do*! Just not with him. He's just not special enough. That's why I broke up with him."

"You did the right thing," I danced inside.

"When I go all the way, I want it to be with someone special."

And she reached over.

And she put her hand on my knee.

And I stopped breathing.

And I looked over to see if she meant what I thought she meant.

And she leaned in.

I leaned in a little, but not too far, because I wasn't sure.

She lifted her eyes.

I couldn't look away.

She kissed me.

She kissed me and I kissed her back and I kissed her again and I kissed her bottom lip and I kissed her top lip and I kissed the corners of both sides of her mouth and she opened her lips for me and I swam in her kisses.

And I didn't know if I was being a good kisser or not, so I jumped up and said something about school tomorrow and ran across the lawn and forgot to climb the tree and ran right through the front door and bounded up the stairs three-at-a-time and didn't sleep.

The next morning, Mom asked me what the ruckus was last night.

"Don't tell anybody," I beamed, "but I think I have a girlfriend."

"Oh really?" My mother would not have been grinning nearly so much if she'd really known what was going on. "Who is this girlfriend?"

"The World's Only Living Nine-Point-Nine, Mom."

"That's what they all say, Son." Her grin grew even bigger. "That's what they all say."

Confessions of a Serial Asshole
– Part Three: Be Cool
(September 1969)

There's no overestimating the amount of confidence a girl like Mila can instill in a young man. Fresh from her kisses, I was feeling ready for conquest that first day at Putnam High School. But the victory was not yet won – not yet.

Fortunately, it's not that hard to figure out a high school clique. I walked into the cafeteria that first morning. I surveyed the scene. I located the two most popular males. I wasn't difficult to spot them. I didn't know their names yet, but I knew I would soon, so I went straight over and sat down next to my two new best friends and started the school year off right.

And it was just exactly that easy!

My racing reputation had preceded me, but not my story. I was free to write it as I saw fit. And with Mila on my side, I was on the fast-track to cool.

I won all my races and set a new school record the first time out. I got invited to join the Putnam Chapter of Phi Sigma Tau fraternity as a legacy and didn't even have to pledge. Roger and I reformed the band, but this time with no Mormons (besides me) in it. Roger played bass, as always, but now Ronny was gone and I was the lead guitarist. We stole our new drummer, Craig Richards, from The Phantoms, one of the most popular bands in the city and we lucked into Little Jimmy Marshall, just barely fifteen, a sweet kid, the younger brother of Mike Marshall – the guitarist in Portland's most legendary band – The Kingsmen. Little Jimmy Marshall became our second guitarist. He played the exact same cherry red Guild Starfire guitar that his older brother Mike had used to record *Louie Louie*.

Little Jimmy Marshall's Mom took a shine to me and used to drive me around in the Jaguar XKE that Mike Marshall bought her with his royalty checks. She even let me drive it before I got my license. She also set us up with a manager – the star-maker and KISN radio personality – Ken Barclay. He said we were the best young group he'd seen in years. He liked our "... raw energy ..." and said that we had a "... certain something." He couldn't put his finger on exactly what it was that we had, but he said we had it. And that sounded very musical to me.

Ken Barclay started getting us gigs – not just church dances, but real gigs. Our first Ken Barclay show was at the Portland International Auto Show at the Exposition Center out by the airport. The stage there was incredible and disorienting.   I couldn't hear what I was used to hearing while playing and I didn't know why. Everything just seemed and sounded wrong to me. But we got through it and everybody said we did great. We played first and were followed by one of Portland's most famous bands, Paul Revere and the Raiders.   They wore their full colonial costumes and did synchronized choreography while they played. And after them, all the way from Motown Records in Detroit, was a new band called Rare Earth. They were fantastic. It was so exciting, I had to pinch myself. I was standing on the side of the stage when Rare Earth kicked off "*Get Ready* 'Cause Here I Come," and I was just so inspired and overwhelmed by it all that I adopted *Get Ready* as my personal theme song, cuz "...Here I come!"

After that show, everybody began to believe we were going to be famous.

The other seriously great thing that happened that fall was that I finally celebrated my sixteenth birthday. I took possession of my long-awaited birthday gift from my grandmother – a 1956 two-tone (Harbor Blue over Nassau Blue) Chevrolet Bel Air 2-door Hardtop that, at last, afforded me the independence I so longed for. I got my driver's license the morning of my 16th-birthday and got my first traffic ticket that same afternoon (for "Driving While Embracing" with Mila). Mila threw me a big bash with all of the cool kids at the Benson Hotel in downtown Portland. My parents were out of town for the weekend. Mila and I became an official item at that party in a very public way, so there'd be no doubt in the minds of any other suitors. She wore my fraternity pin every single day for the rest of high school. We made the rounds at the party and got teen-age-drunk and had a great time.

The next morning I was so hungover that I barely made it to the bus for the George Fox College Cross-Country Invitational, but I staggered up just in time, and in spite of my headache and blurry vision, I took first place. I was off to a good start.

And it only got better.

Mila insisted that my band play all the dances after each football game and nobody argued. Mila was elected both Girls' League President and Homecoming Queen the next two years in-a-row and I was always her escort. I got so I could remove her bra with just two fingers of one hand – in one smooth motion. She liked that. We spent every minute we could parked behind the old Gladstone Drive-in Movie Theater in my big ol' two-tone Chevy exploring each other's bodies.

And I was chosen as Homecoming King after only being at the school for a few short weeks, which I admit caused a hint of resentment from the old guard who had been putting in their time for going on eleven years. (And there were a few whispers about my arrogance growing out of control.) But with Mila on my side, I had nothing to worry about. And I knew it. Even the teachers gave me wide berth. Homework was optional. Class attendance was welcomed, but not required. Putnam High had an open door policy when it came to me and Mila. Sometimes we would drive all the way to The Oregon Coast for lunch and never return. Those were good days.

Yes, High school was going to be awesome. I was pretty sure that life would never be better. I think I may have suspected that it probably wouldn't last forever. It did all seem a little too easy. But if there was going to be a price to pay for all the hubris, I was hoping to push my comeuppance as far down the road as I could.

I wasn't ready to think about that yet.

Not yet.

Not until I had to.

Because I knew, even then, that there was something precious about being young. Everybody said so. Everybody at church and at school. They called us *youth* and said we were special.

"The future belongs to the young," was the prevailing wisdom. But I noticed – even then – that nobody ever bothered to describe what that *future* was going to look like. I wondered what would become of all of us youngsters when the day came that we weren't kids anymore.

It seemed likely to me that we'd probably end up looking a lot like regular, everyday, run-of-the-mill adults.

All you gotta do is look around a bit. When you do, you realize that all the bright, intelligent, fresh-faced, wide-eyed kids in the world just turn into grownups, sooner or later.

I often wondered what happened to that light in their eyes.

It just seemed obvious to me that I should enjoy the flower of my youth while I still could.

Because being young is cool.

Bridge Club/Golf Club
(October 1969)

Amateur psychologists may well have a heyday with this, but the only organization that really mattered at Putnam High School was the unsanctioned, but highly influential, Bridge Club/Golf Club. The popular girls formed Bridge Club, while the highest profile jocks and the boys from the wealthiest families made up Golf Club. We each adopted our same-sex parent's names. I became Bert (my dad's first name) and Mila became Barbara (her mom's) and all the kids in our clique did the same thing. Our closest friends – the insiders and cool kids – called us *Bert* and *Barbara* and we in turn, referred to each of them according to their parents' first names. Some of the more-aware teachers even picked up on it and joined in the fun.

The idea was that when my peers' parents went on their golf outings or got together to play bridge, it was really just an excuse to drink. And of course, we all wanted in on the grown-up fun. That's what we thought it was about – at the time anyway. (Of course, my particular parents didn't golf, or play bridge, or drink for that matter, but my parents were the exception – I was the only Mormon at Putnam High – so I just went with it.) Most of the families with the big houses in Oak Grove in those days had fathers who were executives at Reynolds Aluminum (or some such place) and virtually all of the mothers were stay-at-home moms with plenty of money and time on their hands. Single parents and poor people didn't exist in our neighborhood as far as we could tell.

So our clique formed Bridge Club/Golf Club. We thought it was just an excuse to get together and drink. We met every other weekend at somebody's house – the word would get around as to time and place – and anybody who was anybody would always be there.

Early on that first fall, my parents had another trip planned for out of town. They did that fairly often. (I don't know where they went, but I suspected it had something to do with the fact that there were twelve of us in the family.) When I learned of their plans, I mentioned it to Mila and my house became the next venue for Bridge Club/Golf Club.

And it all went off just fine except for one thing. Unlike the other members of Bridge Club/Golf Club, my parents didn't have a liquor cabinet we could break into. Since we were teenagers, getting enough alcohol for a whole party was sometimes a bit of a challenge. And sure enough, we ran out of booze.

"Come on," Jack Kramer had an idea. "Drive me over to Theissen Store."

Since I was the host, I felt obligated. We went out and piled into my Chevy. Guy Manning joined us.

I drove over to Theissen Store while Jack Kramer explained how he could shoplift a couple jugs of wine, at least. But when we got there, it was much later than we realized and the store was closed. I started to pull away.

"Wait! Back up!" Jack opened the passenger side door.

I backed back into the parking lot.

Jack Kramer ran up to the storefront, grabbed a big metal garbage can and threw it through the plate glass window. The boom of crashing glass echoed and reverberated throughout the neighborhood.

Guy jumped out of my back seat, ran over to Jack, and together they stepped through the shattered glass and into the store. I spun one time in a circle in the parking lot and pulled up next to the broken window.

Jack and Guy came stumbling back out of the hole in the store laughing and toting several jugs of wine each and I sped off back to the party where we enjoyed plenty of wine for the rest of the night.

The next afternoon, after I had sufficiently recovered enough to drive again, I was northbound approaching the Tastee-Freez on SE 42nd Avenue. There was a cop coming southbound toward me and he had his head out of his window waving at the cars ahead of me. There were three or four cars in front and I simply followed them past the cop while he continued to wave. I had never seen a cop do that, so I had no idea what was going on.

As soon as I passed him, he flipped on his lights and his siren and pulled a U-turn and got in behind me. I had just reached the stop sign there on 42nd, so I turned right onto SE King Road and pulled over just past the Tastee-Freez. I didn't know why he pulled me over.

The cop get did not get out of his car.

I watched in my rear-view mirror as he didn't get out of his Police car. He got on the radio instead. I could see him hold the handset up to his mouth and communicate with somebody on the other end. And he just stayed there and kept talking on the radio.

Why wasn't he getting out of his car?

And then I remembered. My Harbor Blue over Nassau Blue Chevy Bel Air 2-door Hard Top was the only one in this part of town. And I was driving it when we robbed Theissen Store last night.

Oh! Shit!

I watched and waited as he sat in his car talking on the radio until I just couldn't stand the waiting any longer.

He still wasn't getting out of his car.

Finally, because I was young and stupid, I got out of my car and went back to his driver's side window to get it over with.

"Why did you pull me over?" I trembled as he stepped out of his door.

"Why do you think?" He looked me over.

"I don't know. I wasn't doing anything." I was shaking all over.

"You must have been doing something." He could tell I was scared.

"I didn't do anything."

I was sure that any second he was going to bring out the handcuffs.

The cop could tell that I was about to confess to something, so he made it his mission to find out what it was. He started peppering me with questions.

Name? Address? Where was I going? Were was I coming from? Whose car is this? How long have I owned it? License? Registration?

I fielded every question the best I could under the circumstances, but I knew it was only a matter of time before I would be bent over the hood of his police car, having my rights read to me. I could feel myself getting ready to confess the whole story about the Theissen Store robbery. The cop must have sensed I was ready to break, because no matter how much I begged him to, he refused to tell me why he had pulled me over.

"Why don't you tell me why you're acting so guilty?" The cop folded his arms.

It was clear that he was going to be able to hold out longer than I was. This was not going to end well.

Finally, I just couldn't take it any more. I opened my mouth and started to say that it wasn't my idea ...

And then the craziest thing happened.

I know it sounds so incredibly outlandish that it's hard to believe, but it really did happen just right then – at that exact moment.

A station wagon pulling a trailer went by going east on SE King Road and just when it got to where the cop and I were standing, the trailer hitch snapped and the trailer came loose from the station wagon.

SE King Road has a pretty good downhill slope right there, so instead of the trailer grinding to a stop, just the opposite happened; it picked up speed as it continued down the hill. Unfettered, with nobody steering it, the trailer traveled an uncontrolled course of it's own. It careened left into oncoming traffic as it gained speed down the hill. The driver of the station wagon must have been surprised, when he saw the trailer passing him on his left, because he hit his brakes. The trailer passed the station wagon and then veered back into the right lane gaining momentum in its dash down the hill with the station wagon following behind. Then incredibly, the station wagon sped up and pulled left into oncoming traffic itself until it got right up beside the trailer and the driver then steered the station wagon right into the left side of the trailer and pushed it off to the right side of the road. The trailer and the station wagon – after performing the world's most unlikely figure-8 maneuver – both came to a sudden crumpled stop when they finally hit a telephone pole together just across SE Home Avenue.

The cop and I both saw the entire thing unfold. We just stood there watching in silence while the whole bizarre scenario played out. Neither of us could believe what we were witnessing.

The cop looked at me. Then he looked down the road at the trailer and the station wagon. Then he looked back at me.

"That looks more important." He shook his head like he had been cheated out of a well-earned victory. He started toward his car and shouted back at me. "There was a lady waiting to cross back there before Tastee-Freez and she had a cross-walk. Stop for pedestrians next time."

I got back in my car and pictured the headlines if I'd been arrested for robbing Theissen Store. It would have killed my father. He was a respected man in our community. It would have been big news. It would have humiliated and embarrassed him.

For the next month, there were signs out in front of Theissen Store offering a $500 reward for information about the robbery. Every single member of Bridge Club/Golf Club knew exactly who did it. But nobody turned us in. My father never knew how close he came to the disgrace, shame and scandal.

New Year's Eve 1969 in the Back Seat of a 1956 Two-Tone (Harbor Blue over Nassau Blue) Chevrolet Bel Air 2-Door Hardtop

Did you come?

I don't know. Did you?

I don't know.

Are you OK?

I think so.

Did it hurt?

It was OK.

You're not a virgin anymore.

I know. Neither are you.

I hope you don't think I planned this.

No, no. I planned it.

What?

I called my sister and she told me what to do.

Oh! Wow! Really?

You're not mad at me?

Mad at you? No, 'course not. It was fun.

Well, it's just that I know it's against the rules and you're not supposed to.

It was worth it.

You liked it?

Are you kidding? You're incredible.

You want to do it again?

Can we?

--

--

--

--

OK, I think you came that time.

Oh! My! God! Yes! Yes, I did. Did you?

I don't know.

Oh, I'm going to do this a lot.

1970 World Tour
(Spring 1970)

So I wrote a song. A silly love song called *Fire in My Heart*.

Verse 1:
    I wonder can you feel it
    It's burning here inside
    You set a Fire in My Heart
    And it's way too hot to hide
    Sooner or later
    There ain't no doubt
    This flame's consumin' me
    And I can't put it out

Chorus:
    There's a Fire in My Heart for you girl
    It's a flame that's burnin' high – I – I
    Got a Fire in My Heart for you, yeah, and it's
    Bringin' tears to my eyes

Mila was convinced I wrote it about her, but honestly, I was just trying to write a hit song. I followed all the rules. I kept it right at exactly three minutes and got to the chorus quickly. I tried to keep it as catchy as possible and followed the form of all the songs on the radio.

I showed it to the guys and we played it for Ken Barclay and he booked a recording studio (my memory is that it was across the Columbia River in Vancouver somewhere) and we went in and made a record.

First we played the guitars, bass and drums without any singing and the engineers up in the control booth (that I don't even remember seeing) mixed it all together and then we went back in and I played piano and sang along twice with what we had played before. Upstairs, they mixed that all together again and then we added some background vocals. There was a Moog synthesizer sitting in the studio with a ton of knobs and patch-cables dangling out of it and I had never seen an actual Moog before, so when we were gathered around the mic doing the background vocals, I asked the engineers up in the booth if we could use the synthesizer on the record.

After a few minutes, a voice came into my headphones and said I could play the Moog as long as I didn't move any of the knobs or cables or settings. So I just used the sound that was already programmed into it and played the melody line from the last two lines of the chorus (which was how we always started the hymns at church). Then I added a Moog solo, instead of the planned guitar solo, just because the Moog was there and I liked the way the sound slid up and down between the notes. So as soon as I played those couple of lines on the synthesizer, the engineers (that I'm pretty sure I never even met) mixed everything all together, and we had our record.

We were giddy with the idea that we were on our way to stardom. I wanted to do *Makin' Me Crazy* – another one of my original songs for the B-side of the record, but Ken Barclay wanted us record a cover version of *For Your Love* by The Yardbirds. And he was our manager. And he was paying for it. So that's what we did.

Ken Barclay took a photo of us holding our guitars and printed up a thousand vinyl 45s with the big hole in the center and he got the DJs at KISN to start playing *Fire in My Heart* and we started getting more and better gigs right away.

The first time I heard my song on the radio was unquestionably the most exhilarating experience of my life. It was indescribably, magically and overwhelmingly fantastic. I felt like a Beatle. (Except that I was the one screaming and clapping and singing along.)

And the second it was over, I couldn't wait till they played it again.

I literally, physically, viscerally ached for them to play it again.

All the kids at school heard it. They sang it to me in the halls when they saw me coming and Miss Bennett, my English teacher, used it in an English lesson. She said it was "... excellent use of metaphor." (I still laugh about that, today.)

Verse 2:
    I wonder if you know that
    Just the way you move
    Can set me off like I got
    Nothin' left to prove
    And before you know it
    I'm burnin' out of control
    I am the furnace
    You are the coal

Chorus:
    There's a Fire in My Heart for you girl
    It's a flame that's burnin' high – I – I
    Got a Fire in My Heart for you, yeah, and it's
    Bringin' tears to my eyes

That's when Ken Barclay set up our first big road trip. It was only ten days and five cities (and one of them was our home town), but we called it our "1970 World Tour." Little Jimmy Marshall's mom even printed up black tour jackets that had our names embroidered on the front and "1970 World Tour" over our logo on the back.

I couldn't believe my parents allowed me to miss more than a week of school, but they did. We started in Seattle and opened a concert there for Tower of Power, who were hugely popular at the time. I thought they were the coolest band I'd ever seen in real life with all the horns and the funk and the groove. This show was way different from the church parties and after-game dances we had been playing before. It was even better than our big showcase with Paul Revere and the Raiders and Rare Earth. The venue was way bigger and there were a lot more lights and it was a much louder and I could hear a whole lot less (in fact, all I could hear was my own guitar – I couldn't hear any vocals at all – not even my own) and there was way more pressure and lots more confusion. But it was also more exciting and invigorating and much less work because there was a stage-crew to do all the setup and heavy lifting.

That first performance went by fast. Really fast. We played every song too fast. I barely breathed between songs as I counted off the next one. All those lights were in my eyes. We got on and we got off.

After the show, Roger talked a girl he met backstage into coming back to the motel with us and he had sex with her in the bed right next to me. I couldn't believe it. I held still and listened, but she didn't seem to care at all that I was there and Roger thought it was the funniest thing ever.

The next night we were back in Portland. We played at the Paramount Theater and opened two shows for Sly and the Family Stone (that's another story altogether) and Mila came to the second show.

We talked Ken Barclay into getting us another motel room (even though we had homes we could go to) and I don't know why, but he agreed. It definitely made the whole experience feel more like being on the road and Mila and I got to do it in a bed, instead of the backseat of my car. Roger and his sometime-girlfriend-Gail were in the room and did it too, but we were in separate beds and we all stayed under the covers and Mila and I tried to stay as quiet as possible.

The next morning was a travel day. I said good-bye to Mila and told her I wished she could come with us. Then we all piled into Ken Barclay's van and headed south.

That was a fun day. We laughed and talked and played the radio and piled in and out of the van at all the rest stops and had a wonderful time dreaming about all the great things we were going to do.

We felt like real rock stars.

I don't remember much about the show in San Francisco except that we opened for Merrilee Rush (who like us, was also from the Pacific Northwest, but unlike us, she had an actual bona fide hit song – Angel of the Morning – on her resume). The two things I do remember about the San Francisco show are 1) the lights were so bright I couldn't see anything at all and 2) the venue was in a part of the city called North Beach.

After the show, Roger brought another girl back to the room. This time though, I left them alone and walked around the neighborhood, because unlike Portland, there was still a whole lot going on in the middle of the night and I was still all wound up and excited after the show.

North Beach in those days was overrun with strip clubs and topless bars and neon signs and graffiti and posters and people all over the place. It was exciting and cool. I saw a girl jump up on the bar at one of the open-air joints and take her shirt off. She wasn't wearing a bra. Everybody cheered. I soaked it all in. There was a barker standing out in front of one of the clubs and he tried to talk me into going inside to see the show. I told him I was only sixteen, but he pulled me in anyway and said, "Just go in and check it out for a few minutes."

I was not prepared for what I saw. I had never imagined such a thing existed. There were men sitting around a large round red velvet table with drinks and cigarettes and in the middle of the table was a guy and a girl having sex. Right there in the middle of the room. The guy was fucking the girl doggie-style and they were both completely naked and all the men were just sitting around watching it happen.

When I got back outside I struck up a conversation with the Barker.

"Did I just see that?" I guess I needed confirmation.

"Get your rocks off, did ya, kid?" He laughed.

"They were really, .. um, .. fucking!" I still couldn't believe it.

"It's a Live Sex Show, kid," he nodded, "it'd be false advertising if they weren't."

"I never saw that before," I had to readjust my bearings.

"Yeah, I figured," the Barker laughed again and we talked for a few minutes and fell into a conversation about all the crazy things to do and see and experience in North Beach.

And then she came outside. The girl. The girl from the red velvet table. The same girl I had just seen naked having sex. She stepped alone, out of the club, out onto the sidewalk, right next to me. She ignored me completely. She didn't even see me, but she stopped and talked to the Barker for a few minutes. And she was cute. She was seriously cute. I couldn't believe it. She looked so different with her clothes on. She was fully dressed like a happy, healthy, young girl in denim and beads with long blonde hair.. She was small and pretty and wholesome-looking and I just couldn't get over how young and alive she was.

I guess I had expected her to be soul-less. But she wasn't soul-less. She seemed normal and happy and beautiful and full of life and I was seriously having to redefine my assumptions and expectations.

When I told the guys about the Live Sex Show the next morning, I found out that not only Roger, but also Craig and Little Jimmy Marshall had likewise brought girls back to the motel that night and that they all ended up in the same room together. And for a while, even in the same bed. Craig said that he had put his thing into both his girl and into Jimmy's girl, so he bragged that he had scored twice. Roger reminded him that he had scored in Seattle and Portland and San Francisco, so that was three.

That left Little Jimmy Marshall with just one – and me – well, I'd only been with Mila in Portland. So they figured my score was zero. They said Mila didn't count, because she was my girlfriend, but I argued that if Roger could count Gail as one of his, then I should be able to count Mila. Besides, I reasoned it didn't matter if it was zero or one. I didn't want to cheat.

That's when they explained the *State Line Rule*. It's not cheating if you're out of state. As long as she was in Oregon and I was in California, it didn't count.

"I don't know," I rationalized away my poor showing on the scoreboard. "I don't want to do anything to hurt Mila."

"Don't tell her," Roger replied. "It won't hurt a bit."

"She'd know." I was sure she would.

"Oh grab yourself by the balls and live a little," Roger challenged.

"Yeah, life's for livin'," even Little Jimmy Marshall piled on.

"How you gonna be a rock star," Craig went for the juggler, "if you're afraid to fuck?"

"I'm not afraid." I was insulted.

"Come on guys," Roger finished up. "Leave Mr. Pussywhipped alone. If he doesn't want to get his balls out, that's just more for the rest of us."

"Fuck you guys," was the best argument I could come up with.

The next two shows were in Los Angeles and that's when the real fun began. Ken Barclay had persuaded (or paid) a disc Jockey at KTLA to spin *Fire in My Heart* for a whole week, so there was a much bigger crowd of girls waiting for us when we got to the show. Some local band (I don't remember their name) opened for us and we played under the brightest lights yet at the Whiskey-a-Go-Go on Sunset Boulevard – right there on the Sunset Strip. It was unreal –

out of this world – incredible! People lined up after the show to get our autographs. That was a first. It was embarrassing in the beginning. I didn't know what to do or say or what to sign. But after a few tries I really got to like it and started having fun with it.

We didn't realize we were changing. Honestly, we had no idea what was happening. We just thought everybody suddenly seemed to love us. Especially the girls. I met a gorgeous brunette with long straight hair a who seemed real interested in me and she had a car and she waited for me after the load out and we drove up into the hills somewhere to a house that she said belonged to her parents, but they weren't home and she didn't have the key.

She got up over the gate and let me in from the inside and she knew exactly how to turn on the hot tub in the back yard. She took off all her clothes and stepped into the warm swirling glowing water, so I took off all my clothes and got in the hot tub too.

She was brown and beautiful. She had no tan lines anywhere and her boobs in the hot tub were big and round and wonderful. She jumped out, naked and wet, and got in the house and came back with some wine and we drank it and I tried to pretend that I did stuff like this all the time. I imagined that this was what living in California was all about. I liked it.

I couldn't get over her boobs. They were so professional. They looked like California, glossy-magazine, air-brushed breasts. They were perfectly-shaped – all brown and round. I would have been happy burying my face in them all night long. But she pulled me out of the hot tub and into the house and onto some home-gym equipment they had in a room there. Then she went down on me, took my dick in her mouth and brought me to orgasm and made me come.

Before I could say anything, she opened her mouth wide to show me my cum. Then she grinned and swallowed it. I couldn't believe it. She went out and got more wine and brought me a towel, but she didn't wear one. She stayed naked and I stared at her wet hair and her amazing breasts while we talked about religion for a while (for some reason, that's the subject that came up) until she started playing with my dick again and I got all excited again and she guided my dick inside her and we had sex right there on the gym equipment. I lasted longer that time and I thought I fucked her pretty good. It was one of the most wonderfully memorable and exciting experiences of my life.

When she drove me back in the morning, I couldn't wait to tell the guys all about Kelly. Her name was Kelly. I relayed the whole incredible story about the hot tub and the wine and all about Kelly's round, professional boobs and the gym equipment and the blow job and I was shocked, surprised and dismayed by their reaction.

"That's not cool," Craig interrupted me, "Mila wouldn't do that to you."

"Yeah," Little Jimmy Marshall judged me as well, "Mila is special. She deserves better."

"But just yesterday," I was aghast, "you guys said that over the State line, it didn't count. You know: the *State Line Rule*. Remember?"

"What she doesn't know won't hurt her." Roger reiterated, but he said it with less conviction than the day before.

"I can't believe you guys," I was more than a little hurt by this sudden change in morality. "You think it's fine for you to do whatever you want, but you want me to miss out on all the fun?"

"If I had a girl like Mila," Craig wished, "I'd treat her better. That's all."

"You say one thing yesterday ... ," I was flabbergasted, "... and what? ... and now today, I'm the bad guy? It's like you have one set of rules for yourselves and another set of rules for me? Well, fuck you and fuck you and fuck you. I'm doing Kelly again tonight. I don't care if you like it or not. She promised she's coming back to the show tonight and I'm not missing out on my chance to fuck her.

And if any of you say anything to Mila — or to anybody else — well that'll just be the end of the group — that's all."

"Relax! Nobody's going to say anything," Roger stepped in. "Don't get so worked up about it. Nobody's going to rat you out."

I looked for Kelly at the show that night. I looked everywhere. I couldn't locate her during the opening act so I told the bouncers to be on the look-out for her. But even with my detailed description of her perfect breasts, they hadn't seen her either.

Then during our set, with the bright lights in my eyes, I wouldn't have been able to tell if she was there or not, anyway. Afterwards, there were more autographs and I still kept expecting to see Kelly at any moment, so when the bouncers came and got us to bring us backstage, I lingered on a little longer than the other guys. Still hoping.

When I eventually got back to the dressing room, Roger was already there. And to my surprise, Kelly was there too. But I was suddenly less-than-thrilled to see her, because she was on her knees and she had Roger's cock in her mouth. I was stunned. I thought she was coming to see me. I stood there for a minute in disbelief, while Roger grinned at me the way he always did when he was misbehaving. I grabbed my guitars, stomped out of the club, foolishly ignored the line of girls still waiting outside, got in the van and demanded to be taken back to the motel. "Now!"

I was hurt.

I knew I shouldn't be. But I was.

It was confusing and embarrassing. But I admit it. It hurt my feelings. I felt like I was being cheated, unfairly, out of something wonderful. I wanted Kelly to fuck me, not Roger. It didn't make any sense at all, but I realized that I actually felt like crying.

About a half-hour later, Roger brought Kelly back to the motel and they could tell that I was pouting.

"Hey! Dude? You want in on this?" Roger invited me for a threesome, pointing to the amazingly-still-lovely-looking, long-haired, big-breasted Kelly, "She's totally cool with it."

"No, you guys go ahead." I didn't know what to do. I was in pain and just couldn't snap out of it.

I went next door to Craig's and Little Jimmy Marshall's room, but they had girls too, so I just sat outside in a plastic chair by the pool and tried to get a grip on my feelings.

After a while, Kelly came outside and found me and said she was sorry and that she didn't have any idea that I cared so much about our night together and that it was just for fun and it didn't mean anything and that she didn't intend to hurt me.

I didn't know what to say. How do you explain your insides to somebody else when you don't understand them yourself?

I knew I shouldn't feel jealous over her. In my brain, I knew she didn't do anything wrong that I hadn't done too. But in my heart, I felt betrayed.

Getting my head and heart to come together was such a struggle. It was like the Mormon Church – in my head, I knew the stories were nonsense, but in my heart, I was having so much trouble letting it all go.

And the guilt just made it all that much harder.

The last two shows were in San Diego. I found a really cool girl there. Her name was Jolene. Jolene introduced me to the concept of foreplay. We walked on the beach and she came to both shows and we made love together for two-and-a-half days and nights.

Roger fucked two girls the first night in San Diego, one the next afternoon, and two more the night of the last show. His final score for the tour was ten. He won the competition.

When we finally got back from our first big road trip in the middle of the night, Ken Barclay informed us that the tour hadn't gone as well as he had hoped – that he was pulling *Fire in my Heart* from rotation on the radio – that we all had some growing up to do – and that he wasn't sure he could continue as our manager.

I never heard *Fire in My Heart* on the radio again.

And that hurt. A lot. It hurt much more than I thought it would. It left a hole in my heart that could only be filled by getting another song on the radio. (And it turned out to be much longer before that happened than I dared imagined at the time).

Mila didn't seem to notice that I was so much better at sex than I had been before. So I just kept right on going to school and to church and to band practice and track practice. I carried on just as if nothing was different – even with that hole in my heart. And I continued sneaking over, in the night, to Mila's warm, welcoming embrace.

Mila got me through.

Mila was even better than before. Our nights together were divine. Glorious. Religious, even. Mila was special. I fell in love with her all over again.

I decided that the only truly morally good thing to do would be for me to keep the truth from her.

I would just have to deal with my guilt privately. I was strong enough. I would have to be.

It couldn't be right – or good – or moral – to tell her the truth.

Why hurt the feelings of someone I loved just because I was still trying to figure things out?

I was the one who broke the rules.

Mila hadn't done anything wrong.

It would have been cruel to hurt her.

And the other part of it was that I didn't regret my California adventures.

Not even a little. How could I?

My nights with Kelly and Jolene were exciting and incredible. I wouldn't trade them for the world. How and why would I feel bad or sorry about something so sensationally wonderful?

I realized that Little Jimmy Marshall, as young and inexperienced as he was, may have had a point when he argued that life was for living.

Besides, technically, I had the *State Line Rule* on my side.

Of course, I knew it was just a made-up rule.

But Hey! Aren't they all?

END OF PART ONE

PART TWO

Somebody Should'a Told You
by Now that Life's Not Fair
(Spring 1970)

Jeff Williams did everything right. He worked hard. Followed the rules. Arrived early. And stayed late. He was the fastest runner at Putnam High School before I got there. After I arrived, he was the second-fastest.

Jeff Williams wanted his spot back. And nobody blamed him.

He was a half-mile specialist so that's where he put his focus. He was no slouch either. He consistently ran sub-2:00-flat, which was pretty impressive for a high-school kid in 1970. The problem was that the faster he ran, the faster he forced me to run. I could always finish a couple steps ahead of him.

So when I took more than a week off to go on a road trip with my band, Jeff saw his opportunity. He ratcheted up his training. He knew I wasn't doing any. And he was right. It was still relatively early in the season and we had the first big highlighted meet coming up. It was only a dual meet with Clackamas High School, but Clackamas had a couple runners that were also sub-2:00 half-milers. The local newspapers got wind of the upcoming contest and made a big deal out of the race, predicting four runners capable of running sub-2:00, which would be a first for a dual meet as far as anyone could remember. The race was billed as the first big test of the season.

Jeff set his goal at the school record, which I had established during the indoor season – 1:55.4. Jeff got together with the coaches in my absence to formulate a plan. He worked out twice-a-day and did speedwork twice a week. He got so he could run quarter-mile repeats at 57-58 seconds each. He jogged between each repeat to keep the rest interval as short as possible. He showed great dedication. Everybody was impressed with his progress. The school record was clearly in jeopardy.

There was a huge turnout the day of the race because of all the newspaper hype about the half-mile. The stands were crowded. There were several reporters gathered before the start and we all heard Jeff proclaim to one of them that he was out for the record. He promised to run faster than 1:54:00.

When the time came, we lined up. The gun went off. And we ran.

And Jeff Williams did in fact run faster than the record. He ran 1:53.9 just like he said he would. The problem was that he didn't even place. He finished fourth. 1.8 seconds before he crossed the finish line, I moved the new school record down to 1:52.1 and Carl Meininger ran 1:52.2 and Ben Jarmin ran 1:52.8 and Jeff never did beat me and never got a school record.

Jeff Williams was a great guy. I genuinely liked him. Everybody liked him. He never did anything wrong and always played by the rules. I sincerely wanted what was best for him. I would have done anything I could to have helped him.

If only he could have basked in even a single shining moment of glorious victory – even just one time – that would have been awesome. It would have made everyone happy. But there was nothing I could do to help him. Because life's not fair.

How To Stop a Train
(Spring 1970)

By all accounts, my father was a born teacher. His pupils loved him and sought him out again and again throughout the years to tell him what a difference he made in their lives. I saw it happen time and time again in parking lots and grocery store aisles. Usually it was a random happenstance meeting – followed by an explosion of emotions and memories. But sometimes former students would go miles out of their way and show up at our front door, just to express their gratitude for my father's influence. It was always heart-warming.

But when Dad got promoted to Principal, everything changed. He was no longer in the classroom. He had to deal with adults – parents and politicians and problems. They didn't typically fall in line for him the way pupils did. He didn't like it.

He found it unrewarding.

And it wore on him.

After the first few years, it became apparent that he was ill-suited for the job. He knew it. And so did everybody else. But he couldn't go back to teaching. He couldn't take the pay cut. By then, we had a new three-story house behind a stone wall in the good part of Oak Grove and a ski boat for vacations and ten hungry kids. Eight of us were growing boys. We consumed massive quantities of food. We drank powdered milk from 50-pound bags and devoured gallons of instant mashed potatoes. Our food bills must have been colossal. Each one of those growing boys (at least) was going to have to on a two-year-mission for the church – and the church didn't pay for that – that was the parents' responsibility. I guess things got pretty tight.

The outlook for the future must have seemed daunting.

In addition to the financial stresses, my dad seriously hated his work. I couldn't believe how often he called in sick. When he did go in, he would come home at the end of the day angry and frustrated.

And it's fair to say that he took it out on us.

If he could find something wrong, there'd be hell to pay. If he couldn't find something wrong, he'd go looking for something wrong, and sure enough – there'd be hell to pay anyway. It was a pattern. We all recognized it.

Sometimes he would even go through the dishes stacked in the cabinets just to see if he could find a dirty one. We always knew he would find something.

The neighbors knew too. They could hear him half-a-block away.

My father was also the type of guy that once he got his anger up, it fed off itself. It cycled higher and higher and got louder and louder and we didn't have to do anything to contribute to it at all. We just sat in silence and endured. His regular rants were pent-up, self-sustaining, serial explosions of vitriol and incrimination.

So those were my teenage years with my dad.

The worst part – the part nobody could hide from – was dinner time. We shared all our meals at a gigantic round table that he had custom-built one summer, because it was hard to find dining tables that seated families of twelve at most local furniture shops. We all sat dutifully in our designated seats at mealtime and hoped that nothing would spark Dad's temper, because once it got going, there was no hope for any of us.

I guess each of us dealt with the stress in our own way, but my brother number five – Vaughn, who was ten-years-old at the time – developed a particularly poor strategy. He began to stutter.

Stuttering was not something my father was going to tolerate. Period.

My father tackled Vaughn's stuttering head-on with all the nuance of a bulldozer rolling downhill. The slightest hint of hesitation in Vaughn's voice brought my dad's wrath immediately down upon him. Right in his face. Every time. My father demanded that Vaughn, through force of sheer willpower alone, conquer the involuntary interruptions in his speech.

One evening (and I can't for the life of me remember the exact word – maybe it was *fork* or *fist* or *food* or something – but it started with an "F," I know that for sure), Vaughn mispronounced a word and Dad jumped on him.

"Say it." Dad demanded.

"Pfth-th-pfth.." Vaughn tried.

"Say it." Dad repeated the command.

"Pfth-th-pfth.." Vaughn repeated back at him.

"Say it!" Dad bellowed a third time and slammed both hands down, shaking the entire table.

"Pfth-th-pfth ... Pfth-th-pfth ... Pfth-th-pth ..." Vaughn began spitting uncontrollably.

"*F!*" My father got red in the face and shouted across the table. "*F! F! F!* Say it!"

Brother number seven, Neal, in first-grade at the time, seated right next to Dad, turned calmly and deliberately to my father's face.

Neal extended his middle finger squarely up in front of Dad's nose and said:

"Fuck you!"

The world stopped turning.

Total silence.

I looked across the table at my fifteen-year-old sister. She looked back at me. We braced ourselves.

But nothing.

Nothing but silence.

We waited for the wrath.

None came.

Dad stopped. It was the first and only time my father's tantrum was ever aborted. In the calmest voice I ever heard come out of him, one that seemed more ominously threatening than his shouting ever did, he turned to Neal.

"Where'd you hear that?"

I looked at my sister again. She looked at me again. She almost grinned. We both knew. I said it every day. Hell, I said it about Dad. Every day. Every single day. I just never said it where he could hear me. And certainly never to his face. Karen knew it. Neal knew it. All the kids knew it. "F?" I was Fucked with a Capital F! We all knew what was coming next. I prepared myself for the fallout.

"Ummm, ... at school," Neal covered for me.

Neal saved his pennies and bought me The Beatles' *Let It Be* album for Christmas that year. We became buddy-boys for the rest of Neal's short life.

Vaughn got over his stutter.

I never got over Neal.

The Campaign
(Spring 1970)

The kid that read the morning announcements over the intercom each morning at Putnam High was a trip. His name was Darrel Taylor. He had an amazing scam going. He wasn't just the school's designated on-air spokesperson, he was also the school drug dealer.

As a way to promote his extracurricular services, Darrel would regularly interrupt his daily recitation of the official shout-outs and schedule-changes for a decidedly unofficial advertisement for a fictitious breakfast cereal – not the real-life *Puffed Wheat*, which was available on grocery shelves – but a magically medicinal product he called: *Puffed Grass*.

He'd slip into his best huckster vocal imitation:

"Are you feeling low? Life got you down? No worries my friends. Now, there's *Puffed Grass*. Get yours today. It's fortified with nine essential vitamins and minerals. It'll cure what ails you. All your problems will – poof – disappear in a puff of smoke. It's ninety-nine and forty-four-one-hundredths percent pure. Nine out of ten doctors who puff grass recommend *Puffed Grass* for their patients who puff grass."

Each day it was different and often very creative. But it was always hilarious, because he always got away with it. To this day I don't know if the administration and the teachers were really that clueless, or if at least some of them knew what was up, but didn't say anything because they were just as entertained by it as we were.

I was a big fan of Darrel Taylor and his daily scam even though we ran in very different circles – he with the theater geeks and stoners and I with the jocks and cool kids. But Darrel and I butted heads in a big way when they put out the call for nominations for next year's Student Government.

Naturally, I finagled it so I was nominated for Student Body President. My competition, it turned out, was Darrel Taylor.

I calculated that Darrel had a huge advantage over me in that he commanded the entire school's undivided attention over the intercom every morning. And sure enough, right out of the gate he pushed his own clever Student Body President advertisements into each day's program in addition to his pitches for *Puffed Grass*.

This was going to be more of a challenge than I'd bargained for.

And I couldn't afford to lose.

Losing was not an option.

I couldn't lose face. I couldn't risk losing status. I simply could not lose the election. Even the remote possibility of losing was just not something I was willing to mess around with.

Luckily, in my World Problems class, we had just finished a unit on propaganda. Mr. Heinz identified five major propaganda techniques and made us memorize them:

1) Glittering Generalities
2) Transfer
3) Name Calling
4) Testimonial
5) Band Wagon

So I thought since propaganda seems to work so well for governments and corporations, why couldn't it get me what I wanted too?

I decided I needed to put the full list of established strategies to work on my side. I recognized that I wouldn't carry the druggie vote and that the upperclassmen were more likely to be tuned into Darrel's world view than the younger kids. But the freshman and sophomore classes were larger than the other two, so I decided to go with the numbers and concentrate my campaign on the less-sophisticated voters. I went to work to put my new understanding of propaganda techniques to use as best I could.

First we came up with a simple slogan: *Run With Reed.* We paired it with photographs of my claim to fame – me winning races – and plastered posters all over the school. With each photo, in addition to our slogan, we also added a (1) *glittering generality* one word each: *Dedication* or *Perseverance* or *Integrity.*

The propaganda principle of (2) *transfer* was easy and obvious. We needed an immediately recognizable and powerful symbol to associate with my campaign, so we added the five Olympic rings to all my posters, leaflets and advertisements. I found a red, white and blue USA Olympic Team track jacket at McMillan's Sporting Goods Store in West Lynn and started wearing it to school every day in order to remind everyone that I was destined for greatness.

Next, with the help of Mila and the gang from Bridge Club/Golf Club, we began a systemized (3) *name-calling* campaign. We considered using "Darrel the Druggie" or "Drug Dealer Darrel," but those monikers didn't ring out to my ear the way I needed them to. And besides, we didn't really want to expose Darryl's Puffed Grass scam, we just wanted to win the election. So we decided to use his second-biggest asset against him instead.

Darrel Taylor always won the lead role in all the school plays and he was clearly the top dog in the Drama Department, so we just decided to call him "Drama Darrel," because the two words sounded funny and derogatory at the same time – almost like a single-humped camel. And it worked. It was surprisingly easy to get people to repeat it. We just kept at it. We all referred to him as *Drama Darrel* from then on. And it didn't take long until it caught on. Soon you could hear it all over the halls.

Next, I needed a (4) *testimonial.* I put a lot of thought into to that one. The way the campaign worked was that we'd hold a big assembly just before Election Day. Each candidate would have a designated Campaign Manager speak to the whole school about his or her sterling qualifications. Only then would the actual candidate be allowed to step to the podium. So I needed the most respected, like-able, believable person in the school. That was easy. Mark Goodman was the outgoing student Body President and Senior Class Valedictorian. He had the requisite authority, the good looks, the reputation, and for a nice topping, had just been accepted to Harvard – and everybody knew it.

The problem was that I wanted him to take all of his clothes off during his speech – in front of the entire school. I wanted him to strip all the way down to his boxers. He thought such a stunt was beneath his dignity. He didn't want to do it.

I was convinced that it was an outrageously stupendous idea. I knew Drama Darrel's speech would likely be very effective – he was an experienced entertainer and undeniably accomplished at getting the attention of a crowd. I needed something completely over the top. I was sure the most respected, celebrated and successful student in the entire school actually stripping down to his skivvies while he delivered his speech would get everyone's attention. I was positive it would be the one thing everybody would talk about after the assembly. So I kept after Mark Goodman. I badgered him about the idea every day. It wasn't until the actual day of the assembly that he finally relented and agreed to do it.

My last – and most important – propaganda strategy was (5) the *bandwagon* technique. I had to convince the freshmen and sophomores that everybody was going to vote for me. I decided to make my argument with sights and sounds. Luckily I was going to be the last to speak. Drama Darrel got the bad draw. He and his campaign manager had to go first.

I had my band set up and ready to go behind the curtains the day of the assembly (with my former-band-mate Ronny taking my place on guitar). I had composed a special rock-n-roll song for the occasion entitled *Run With Reed*. Our amplifiers were set at full volume. My old friend from Milwaukie High School, Jerry Gold borrowed two giant real-life foghorns from his father's tugboat (I don't know if you've ever stood next to an actual foghorn when it went off, but indoors, foghorns are what scientists call: "... really, really loud"). We placed one foghorn on each side of the auditorium. The guys and girls from Bridge Club/Golf Club spent a week and half tearing up newspapers and we strategically placed confederates ready to scream and throw confetti throughout the audience. Everything was set to go.

Darrel's Campaign manager went first and she really played into our hands. She just spoke. She said glowing things – as expected – about Darrel. She made a few clever references to his morning announcements (that went right over the heads of my target audience, the underclassmen), but her speech was mostly forgettable.

Next up was Darrel. He gave a rather standard stump speech as well, which totally surprised and delighted me. He basically just detailed a list of standard campaign promises, with one amazing exception. The one thing he said that I – and everyone else – did take note of was that he seriously raised the stakes of the contest. He declared that he was so confident of victory that he promised he would never set foot in school again if he didn't win the election.

It seemed our name-calling campaign had been far more successful than we could have hope for. Even Darrel Taylor had begun to think of himself as *Drama Darrel*.

My campaign manager was next. And he totally pulled it off. As Mark began speaking, he loosened his tie. As he continued, he made a point of removing his tie. Then he slipped his jacket off and let it fall to the floor.

When he started unbuttoning his shirt, his words no longer mattered.

The excitement in the room mounted as each article of clothing collapsed to the floor. Nervous laughter spread through the auditorium. Mark kept right on going. He spoke just as if he were completely serious, all the while shedding yet another piece of clothing. He kicked off his shoes, pulled his t-shirt over his head and finally loosened his belt to the growing roars of the room. He finished with a flurry and shouted "Run with Reed" as he dropped his pants. When he bent over to retrieve his discarded wardrobe from the floor, he had a *Run With Reed* patch sewn to the butt of his boxers.

We had their attention.

When the Principal announced my name, I stood. The curtains parted and the band kicked off with a big fat drum-fill. The guitars and foghorns kicked in at the same time. The cacophony was deafening. Then the confetti began to rain and the cheering commenced. It looked and sounded more like a victory celebration than a campaign speech.

When the roar eventually subsided, I gave it my best Mormon sincerity and repeated our glittering generalities as often and succinctly as possible with, ".. dedication, perseverance, and integrity." And sat down.

Darrel kept his promise and never showed his face at school again.

The Fight
(Spring 1970)

Back five years before – back in the seventh-grade – when I used to get bullied and harassed at the bus stop – and then whine about it – my dad would always say:

"You better learn to fight, then."

My dad even showed me how to keep my hands up and hold my thumbs on the outside of my fists – never on the inside – so as not to injure myself. He explained that holding my thumbs on the outside would also help my fists pack more of a wallop.

But I never put his advice to any use at all. That just wasn't me. I didn't want to fight. I seriously didn't. And I sure-as-hell didn't want to get hit – or beat up. So I learned the art of avoiding conflict. It became a central part of my skill-set and I practiced it at every turn. With exactly one exception – the one and only fight (if you can call it that) of my entire life:

During my campaign for Student Body President my junior year, there was one kid I just could not win over, no matter how I tried. Unfortunately for me, he was the biggest and meanest – by far – kid in school. The major reason he couldn't stand me was that he had a serious crush on Mila. But he also disliked me because my running exploits had garnered so much attention. He was the other kid the local newspapers had marked for future athletic fame. The funny thing was that that they were right about him. (He went on to become a first-round draft pick in the NFL and got himself a Super Bowl ring.)

His name was Jim Stark and he was All-State in football since his freshman year. He won the State Championship in wrestling in the Heavyweight Class as a sophomore. And as a junior, he set a national high school record in the Discuss Throw that remained unmatched for almost twenty years. He stood 6'7" and weighed 285 pounds. The guy was a monster. There was a rumor going around every other school in the state that Jim Stark had a big red Superman "S" tattooed on his chest. He didn't (we knew because we showered with him), but we let everybody else believe it, because it was good strategy for our sports teams.

Jim Stark resented me big time and I knew it. He made it obvious to everyone (including Mila) that he thought Mila should be with him – not with me. So after a few feeble attempts to make nice and win him over – which utterly failed – I simply made it my business to stay out of his way. That worked out pretty well most of the time (like I said, I'd become quite skilled at conflict-avoidance). But the day before the big vote for Student Body President, Jim decided to try to influence the outcome of the election.

I was sitting with the popular kids at our designated table in the cafeteria enjoying my pre-election-day-lunch. Jim walked by behind me with a fresh big bowl of chocolate dessert he'd just collected from the Lunch Lady. As he passed, Jim dumped the entire bowlful of creamy cold goop on my head and rubbed it around, laughing.

I didn't react. I was motivated entirely by self-preservation. I let him have his fun. What else could I do? As soon as he was satisfied and moved on, I began patting my face and head with the few napkins available at the table to the sound of the scattered whispers and twitters that sprung up in several corners of the cafeteria.

The available napkin supply turned out to be insufficient for the task at hand, so although I was mortified by the public display, I got up and took the long humiliating trek to the washroom where I stuck my head under the sink.

I rinsed and rinsed until I thought most of the chocolate was gone and then I tried to clean up my collar and shoulders from the drippings. I held my head under two wall-mounted blow-driers and brushed and fixed my hair with my fingers until I was satisfied that I looked somewhat respectable again.

But when I exited the washroom, Jim was waiting.

Positioned between me and my return to the wide open cafeteria, with the entire student body watching, Jim Stark stood, hands on hips, defying my return to normality. Denying me access to my dignity.

I couldn't retreat back into the washroom. That would have been suicide. So I did what I always did – I tried to play it off.

"C'mon Jim, you had your fun," I attempted to walk by him in the most non-threatening way possible.

He pushed me.

He pushed me back with such force that it surprised and scared me. I knew he was big, but I had never imagined, even with his obvious physical strength, that he was capable of such force. I flew backwards like a crumpled wad of paper – a good ten feet at least. I very nearly went down, but luckily landed on my feet and looked up.

And here he came.

I tried to brace myself. He was coming. I didn't want to go down. ("Here he comes. He's almost here. Keep your feet on the ground. Don't go down.")

He pushed me again. Even harder. This time I crashed back into the wall behind me and would have fallen for sure, but he grabbed me by my left and right collar and lifted me up into the air over his head and pinned me against the wall with my feet dangling helplessly below me.

I was at his mercy. I tried to wriggle free, but I was powerless. So I stopped struggling.

And that's when I saw it.

I looked out over the top of Jim's head as he held me suspended up against the wall and I saw it.

Every eye in the cafeteria – every single eye – hundreds of them – in captivated pairs – every single eye was trained directly and intensely on me. I had never been more the center of more attention in my life. This moment was going to define me in all those eyes. And I knew it.

That's all it took.

I snapped.

Suddenly fearless. No fear of any kind. None whatsoever. No regard for consequences. I started hitting Jim Stark. With both fists. Right in his face. As hard as I could. Left, right, left, right, left, right, again, and again, and again. I got at least twenty-seven swings in while he held me there. He was unfazed by my impotent barrage. He simply held me up while I pounded away as fast and as hard as I could. He held me by my neck and I wailed at his face with all my might.

Teachers came running. Several of them surrounded us shouting for us to stop. I kept right on pummeling with all my might. Jim's grip didn't loosen and I could feel welts coming up on both sides of my neck from where he was holding me. So I continued swinging just as hard as I could, inflicting no damage whatsoever.

The shouting and the holding and the hitting continued.

I was going to swing away as long as he let me.

Without warning – and without ever hitting me – even once – Jim put me down. He turned to his left and started toward the exit. I started after him. With his hands off my neck, I found my voice.

"You fuckin' son-of-a-bitch," I stayed with him every step as he walked steadily down the hallway.

"You touch me again and I'll fuckin' kill you," I barked at him inches from his ear as we walked together towards the doors. We both completely ignored the teachers who were trying to get us to stop.

Jim kept moving. So so did I. And I didn't let up.

"You so much as talk to Mila again or come near me again...," I was all adrenaline – there was no such thing as fear – only unmitigated rage. "I will take you out, you fuckin' asshole. I will take you out. Do you hear me?"

And I continued like that – non-stop – all the way out to the parking lot with more and more teachers, administrators and students following behind. Everybody thought there was going to be more fireworks once we got outside, but the only explosions were the ones coming out of my mouth. And I unleashed them in a rapid-fire torrent even more blindly than the way I had swung my puny fists at Jim's face.

Jim Stark just kept walking while I badgered him with insults and hollow threats all the way out to his car. He found his keys, opened his door, got in his car and drove away and never came back to school – ever. (The next day, he transferred to a private school. He went on to play football at USC and had a 13-year NFL career, before becoming a professional wrestler.)

Jim just drove away.

He left me standing in the parking lot by myself.

Not sure what to do next, I tried to gather my composure. A large crowd had followed us outside. All those eyes were all still watching. I finally turned to face them and the first teacher to me said:

"I can't believe you stood up to Jim Stark."

That was the moment I realized that his plan had backfired.

I was elected Student Body President the next day in a landslide. I never knew if Drama Darrel had put him up to it or not, because none of us ever saw either of them again – not in high school anyway.

We did, of course, all see Jim on TV on Saturday and Sunday afternoons for the better part of the next two decades. And every single time we saw him, we all remembered fondly that we went to high school with him. It is highly unlikely however that anybody from the class of '71 (other than myself of course), ever remembered who was elected Student Body President that spring, because the day high school ended – and likely even before that – it meant less than nothing.

We Damn Near Killed Timmy
(Summer 1970)

It's possible, I guess, that my parents were trying somehow to make it up to me. (They had after all, grounded me for the entire summer after my sophomore year – and they had stuck to it). But the next summer, after my junior year, they totally overcompensated and went the other way.

The day after school got out, they let me take our ski boat and the family station wagon (along with six of my best friends) to Pelton Dam in central Oregon. FOR A WEEK! (The station wagon had the trailer hitch, so I had to leave my car for Mom to get around in – I knew she wasn't going to do anything to hurt it – I have no idea why she thought the same thing about me.)

I honestly don't know why they trusted the sixteen-year-old-me with all that freedom. It's still hard for me to believe it. But they did. As soon as we pulled away from the house, after promising to be good, we stopped and bought several cases of beer. Timmy Tucker had robbed a shitload of wine from the restaurant where he worked as a busboy, so between the beer and wine, we figured we were set.

I got the station wagon up to a hundred-and-seven on a back road, which I think was a record at the time for towing a boat. We found the sweetest campsite on the banks of the reservoir, right behind the dam, and got the boat in the water and began the drinking. And it lasted all week long.

Mila snuck up the second night with a bunch of the girls from Bridge Club and summertime was a full go. It was all sex and drinking and fun and music and hanging out until we passed out and, oh yeah, getting up in the morning and going water-skiing with hangovers.

That's when I learned that the best thing for a hangover is more beer. I was informed by the guys in Golf Club that it's called the Hair of the Dog Rule. And it totally works.

The rest of the rules though, just didn't seem to matter very much that week. For example, you're supposed to have a spotter in the boat whenever you're towing a skier. The driver is supposed to safely navigate the lake while the spotter keeps his eye on the person being pulled behind. The problem with that, for us, was that during the daylight hours, when the sun was up, the girls would all lay out on the ski dock in their bikinis. So, after the first day, none of the guys wanted to get in the boat. Fine. We went without a spotter on most runs.

Since it was my family's boat, and since I had the most skiing experience, I felt perfectly authorized to be the one that did the most showing off. I made a very public pledge to ski the whole week without getting wet. And I did. It was easy. I'd jump off the dock from a standing start. (My buddy Ted would drive the boat whenever I skied.) I'd set some slack in the tow rope and have Ted slowly idle away from the dock. Then just when there was the right number of loops of nylon line laying loose on the surface, I'd yell "Hit it!"

Ted would slam the throttle forward and the slack would unreel away and I'd time my jump just right. I'd land with my one ski flat on the surface and slip my rear foot into the back binding of the ski and slalom off. I could cut through that perfectly flat calm water behind the dam and swing wide and gather enough tension in the ski rope to pull up and fly back to the other side and jump high over the wake, landing safely and athletically on the placid glass of the other side. I even knew several mid-air tricks that I was confident I could perform (even while impaired). So I showed off a lot. As soon as I figured I'd entertained everyone quite enough, I'd signal for Ted to return back by the dock.

On the way in, I'd head right for the girls at top speed, throw the rope away and coast smooth and sweet right up to the dock, wait until just the last second, turn my ski sideways and sit down on the dock with my trunks still dry. And with only minimal residual spray on my hair and shoulders, which I would shake off on whoever happened to be closest.

The best trick I did though was when I only pretended to come back in.

For this trick, I'd signal to Ted for a pass by the dock, and I'd swing way wide to gather speed and momentum and to make the rope as taught as possible, but instead of letting go of the rope, I'd dig my fin (along with the entire tail of the ski) down deep below the surface and throw a massive wall of water up onto the sunbathers. I got so I could cover every square inch of the dock with a drenching. It was awesome fun.

What I didn't know was that Timmy Tucker was watching these antics and secretly planning his revenge.

If he'd have confided his plan to me, I'd have explained that you can't spray the dock with two skis (and Timmy was definitely a two-skis-only-skier). In order to get a good wall up, you have to dig the big fin (I skied on an O'Brien slalom ski with an oversized fin) plus most of the back-half of the ski down deep. There's just no possible way to get that much leverage with two skis flat on the surface, no matter how much you try to shift your weight.

But Timmy didn't tell me his plan. So I didn't tell him it wouldn't work. And when it was Timmy's turn to ski, I was driving the boat. Without a spotter.

You can't really do a standing start on two skis, so Timmy sat on the edge of the dock with his two skies dangling below him and yelled "Hit it!" He got up just fine. He was a boring skier. I steered a circuit of the lake and wished my headache would go away and took a couple more sips from the beer can I had stashed beneath the instrument panel.

I kept one eye on Timmy and one eye on the rest of the lake. I saw him signal. I thought he was done. I thought he meant for me to take him back to the dock to finish his run.

As I approached the dock at about 35-miles-per-hour, there was another boat, just past the dock, about a boat length from it, waiting to pull away, so I motioned for Timmy to swing wide over to the dock, while I set a course just out of the way of the bow of the waiting boat. I was unaware that Tim had other plans. I thought he was going to let go.

But Timmy had no intention of letting go.

I didn't know that, so I just carried on. As I approached, I put my beer down so nobody dockside would see it, because I didn't know who was in the other boat. I passed by just as planned – no problem. But Timmy didn't let go. He held on. He was so focused on why his skis wouldn't spray as he flew by the dock at full speed that he didn't even see the idling boat directly in front of him. My ski rope crossed over the bow of the other boat and then over its windshield as it lay low in the water. Meanwhile, Tim – still attached to the other end of my ski-line – was headed directly at the waiting vessel.

All I saw was the splash explosion of water and two skis soaring straight up high into the air. Both skis spun around as they ascended upwards into the sky. They stalled for a moment at their respective apogees before spinning back and plunging down into the lake.

Oh! Shit!

My first thought was that my father was going to kill me.

I didn't know what happened to Timmy and I didn't want to know. I didn't even want to go back and look. I assumed the worst. And I thought my life was over.

Not Timmy's! Mine!

Before I even got the throttle pulled back, I'd already figured out that if Timmy was dead, there'd be no way to explain it away. All the drinking and all the not-spotting and all the rule-breaking would be found out.

Wait!

Maybe we could get rid of the beers, before the cops came. Maybe I could get Ted to say he was in the boat with me. Would everybody go along? What if somebody talked? And what about the other boat? What had they seen? What did they know? Would they be cool? Did they even survive? Probably not. I was probably fucked. My dad was going to kill me dead. I almost didn't even turn around just to avoid coming face to face with the verdict.

Alone in the boat, with only my limited imaginary scenarios to converse with, I fairly quickly worked out that I would have to go back to the dock sooner or later. So I slowed to a crawl, pivoted, and reluctantly steered back to where the strange boat was still idling a few feet from the old wooden dock. Dreading what I was about to witness.

When I got there, everybody was laughing.

It turned out that Timmy had looked up at the last split-second and seen the boat. He planted his ass down on the water and the tips of his skis popped up into the air. Since Timmy was still holding on tight to the ski handles when the collision occurred, the taught line had popped him right out of his skis, launching both of them flying straight up into the sky and pulling Timmy (still holding on tight to the ski rope) right up, over, and across the other boat where he landed safely – completely unharmed – in the warm water on the other side. I hadn't seen him in the water, because I was watching the flight of the skis. Or maybe because I'd had a little too much to drink.

The people in the other boat were doing the loudest laughing. They thought it was the funniest thing they'd ever seen. They didn't even care about the scratches Timmy's skis left on the port side of their boat, which to my great relief, were not nearly as bad as I expected them to be.

I got my father's ski boat tied to the dock and asked Mila to grab me another beer.

I spent the rest of the week having sleeping-bag-sex with Mila, sampling different wines from exotic regions of the world, and in the mornings, treating my hangovers with *Hair of the Dog* and trying to teach Timmy how to ski on just one ski.

Integrity is Important
(December 1970)

The only skirmish of any significance that Mila and I experienced during our almost two years of going steady (first day of junior year to last day of senior year) happened at the Lloyd Center in northeast Portland during our senior year, just before Christmas of 1970.

"Where've you been?" She seemed a little miffed, "we said we'd meet above the skating rink at 3:15."

"Yes, I know," I explained, "the line was long. I was trying to get here."

"Well, what'd you get?" She seemed almost over it already.

I handed her my shopping bag.

"What's this?" She pulled out a trinket.

"It's a barrette, you know, it goes in your hair."

"I know what a barrette is. Who's it for? The baby? He's a boy!" Mila looked perplexed.

"It's for Karen, of course," I explained.

"What? She's fifteen. She doesn't want a pink barrette. Oh My God! What are you thinking?"

Maybe Mila wasn't quite over me being late, after all.

"I don't know what she wants. I'm not a girl," I looked around for an exit.

"That's not the point," Mila declared. "How much did this cost? 19 cents?"

"About that," I guessed.

"What? What else did you get?" She began digging through my single bag of gifts to see what other evidence of my incompetence she could discover.

"You don't understand," I had a feeling where this was headed.

"This is all crap," was her verdict. "This is just a bunch of junk. An army man? A top? A plastic car? There's nothing in here that cost more than a dollar. What are you doing?"

"You don't understand," I plead my case, "there are twelve of us, counting Mom and Dad. We got ten kids in my family. For you, it's just you and your sister. I gotta buy presents for eleven other people just in my family alone. And that doesn't count you," I tried to get on her good side. "I'm saving my money for something nice for you."

"Don't you worry about me," Mila was unmoved. "How much money did you plan on spending for your family?"

"Well, I don't have that much to spend. And there are so many."

"But you had all those shows the first two weeks of December. You played two nights at the D-Street Corral and you played two proms plus that Christmas party. You said you were going to make good money this year."

"Well, that party didn't pay that much, but the proms paid pretty good," I admitted.

"What happened to all that?"

"That money is promised for something else." I knew I was in trouble now.

"Not for me. It better not be for me." She was adamant. "You're not going to treat your family this way and then blame it on me."

"No, no it's not for you," I should have changed the subject, but I didn't.

"What then?" She raised her eyebrows.

I took a deep breath. "I promised Guy Manning's dad I would buy his guitar. He has a 1953 Gibson Les Paul Gold Top that he bought brand new from a shop in San Francisco when he got back from the Korean War. It's been in its original case under his bed for its whole life. It's a beautiful guitar and he said he would sell it to me for $300.00. I promised him I'd buy it."

"What? A guitar? You already have a guitar." Mila couldn't believe it. "You're not really that selfish, are you?"

"But it's a 1953 Gibson Les Paul Gold Top with the original P-90 pickups and .."

"I don't care if it's solid gold and plays itself," she was unmoved, "you can't treat people this way."

"But it's the deal of a lifetime. It's an absolute dream guitar. You don't understand."

"You're right. I don't understand." Mila was getting angry now. "I don't even know who you are. How could you do something like this?"

"What? What'd I do?" I hoped I could still wriggle out of it. "So I spend a little less on everybody else and take advantage of a once-in-a-lifetime opportunity. I can't pass it up. I can't. You just don't get it."

"No. *YOU* don't get it." She shoved the shopping bag back at me. "Now take all this cheap crap back where you got it and try again. And try to be a little less selfish this time. If you think you can be."

"But Mila." I still hoped I could reason with her.

"Wait! Are those roasted nuts in your pocket?"

"They smelled so good." I was busted.

"I don't believe you!" It was official. Now she was angry. "You bought roasted nuts for yourself and worthless bobbles for everyone else? You've seriously got some growing up to do, my love." Now, go return this junk." She folded her arms. "I'll be here when you get back."

"I can't take it back. I gave my word. I told Guy's dad I would give him the money tomorrow at church." I stayed right where I was.

"You better take it back."

"I can't Mila. I gave my word."

I didn't speak my next thought out loud to her. I didn't dare. But there was no way on earth I was going to give in to her demands.

Because to be honest, it wasn't about giving my word. Or keeping my word either.

I had to have that guitar.

If Mila was mad about it, well, that wasn't fun, but it was a price I was willing to pay. I couldn't make her understand, so there was no point in trying. I knew she would get over it. I would just stand firm on the "I gave my word" excuse. That way, my integrity would still be intact. And we would survive. It was a whole lot better than missing out on a 1953 Gibson Les Paul Gold Top in its original case.

I bought Mila a tiny white-gold heart on a chain with the world's smallest diamondelle embedded for $36.00 and I gave Guy's dad $300.00 cash at church the next day. He had my Gold Top Les Paul guitar in his trunk.

I loved that guitar.

The Inverse Square Law
(Winter 1971)

I wouldn't say that all schooling is a complete waste of time. I learned a few things in school – my times-tables, the names of some of the travelers who accompanied Lewis and Clark and, as I've already mentioned, a few useful propaganda techniques. The last actually practical thing I learned in a classroom was the idea that electricity wasn't invented; it was discovered.

It turns out that electricity has been around since long before humans ever knew anything about it. And one of the interesting things about electricity is that it doesn't care whether you believe in it, or not.

I learned that from Mr. Cox, my high school physics teacher. I also learned a thing or two from him that I'm pretty sure he didn't intend to teach.

Mr. Cox was great. He was funny and fun. He was easily my favorite teacher. I remember one day Mr. Cox tip-toed over to our classroom door and taped a large sheet of black construction paper over the window so nobody could see inside. Then he turned to us and pressed his index finger to his lips to tell us to sssshhhhhh!

We all watched as he took the fire extinguisher down from the wall, pulled the pin out of the handle, climbed on a wheeled cart, and pulled the trigger.

White foam exploded out of the extinguisher and the cart scooted our grinning physics teacher across the room like he was riding a slow-motion rocket. Mr Cox was always doing stuff like that. He said it was a demonstration of Newton's Third Law. I liked it better as a demonstration of how much fun it is to break the rules.

"Don't try this at home, kids," he'd always say.

Sometimes, he would inhale helium and say, "Don't try this at home" in a funny high-pitched voice just to make us all laugh.

Once, Mr. Cox mixed up some potassium nitrate and sugar in a beaker and ignited it. It filled our classroom with so much smoke that we had to open all the windows and I think he got in trouble for that one.

As soon as we got the room clear enough to breathe again, he reminded us: "Don't try this at home."

Mr. Cox was pretty damned entertaining. I remember another day, he promised us he was going to defy gravity. He tore up some small bits of paper and laid them on his desk. Then he rubbed a ballon all over his head and messed his hair all up. When he held the balloon out over the bits of paper, the pieces began dancing and rising up toward the balloon, defying gravity.

It wasn't exactly his best trick ever, but I noticed that he neglected to tell us to not try this at home. So I reminded him.

"Don't try this at home?" I prompted.

His response seemed strange at the time.

"Knock yourself out. Defy gravity all you want – wherever you want – whenever you want. Gravity won't care," he replied.

"Huh?"

"Gravity doesn't care whether you defy it or not. Gravity doesn't need you. Gravity's going to be just fine."

"I was only, ... Wait ... I don't think I know what you mean," I was confused.

"How many inches in a foot?" He asked me out of the blue.

"Um, ... twelve," I got it right.

"And how many feet in a yard?"

"Three," I still didn't see his point, but I was sure I was passing the test.

"Why?" He asked.

"Why what?"

"Why are there twelve inches in a foot? Why not fifteen? Or thirty-seven?"

"I don't know. Tell me," now I wanted to know.

"Because we made it up," he surprised me.

"What?"

"We made it up," he repeated. "We just simply made it up. And the funny part is that it doesn't even make sense. It's clunky and difficult and completely arbitrary. Why should there be 5,280 feet in a mile? There doesn't have to be. That's the answer."

"But the Metric System makes sense," I tried to impress him with my studiousness, "it's all based on tens."

"The Metric System is at least consistent and infinitely more useful, but even the Metric System is also just a man-made set of arbitrary standards that we just made up," he undercut my point.

"So what are you saying?" I still wasn't connecting the dots.

"I'm saying that it's our job as teachers to make sure you know the conventions – the rules – the made-up bits – so you can graduate and go to college and go out into the world and become good citizens." Mr. Cox paused for a moment as if he was trying to work something out in his head and then he returned to me, and patted me on the head, and said:

"Gravity's going to be just fine. It's you we're all worried about."

"Well," I thought about it, "if we're making things up, why don't we make them easier?"

"You mean make Pi just be 3.0 instead of 3.14159.... and so on to infinity?"

"Yes," I pretended I'd thought of that, "that's exactly what I mean."

"Because we didn't make Pi up," he explained, "we figured it out. Or more accurately, we're still figuring it out. Pi lives in the Universe. Pi doesn't need us. We need it. We're stuck with it the way it is, whether we like it or not."

"So some things are real parts of the Universe and other things are just made up?" I wondered aloud.

Mr. Cox clarified, "Look! It's like the Inverse Square Law – that's an even better example. The Inverse Square Law is a natural feature of the Universe across multiple phenomena – gravity, light, sound and electrostatic force, which is what I just showed you with the balloon and the paper – and the point is that nobody invented it. It's just a beautiful, wonderful, consistent feature of the way the Universe actually works. It just is."

"Hmmmm," I was trying to understand, "so how do we know the difference between the way the world really works and the rules we just made up?"

"Requirements," he replied.

"Requirements? I don't ..." I wasn't following again.

"Do some of your teachers wear suits and ties while some of your teachers wear dresses?" He took another tack.

"Yes," but I still didn't see.

"Who wears ties?" He waited for the answer.

"The men teachers wear ties," I was trying to figure it out.

"Why?"

"Ummm, cuz they're supposed to?" I guessed. "Is it a rule?"

"It's a requirement," he explained, "it's a societal requirement that has been codified into the formal rules for Putnam High School."

"I didn't know." I hadn't ever thought about it.

"What would happen if tomorrow the women teachers wore suits and ties and the men teachers wore dresses?"

"You'd probably get called in to the Principal's office," I laughed at the idea.

"Does the Inverse Square Law come with requirements?" He raised his eyebrows. "Does it care whether you behave in a certain way or not? Or believe in it or not?"

"Ummm. No."

"That's the difference."

Mr. Cox was definitely my favorite teacher.

My Close Encounter with Clairvoyance
(May 1971)

It was the City Championships – my senior year. And I was nervous. So nervous in fact, that during my warm-up, I scurried over several times into the bushes to throw up. I did not feel good.

The experts were saying that I hadn't panned out – that my times in the mile hadn't improved – that I could be beaten. They were saying that two of my competitors – Carl Meininger from Clackamas and Scott Johnson from Centennial – both had a real good shot at taking the mile crown from me; they had both improved, while I hadn't. They were getting closer to me every week. It was true. I knew it was going to be tough. And even though the top two finishers would go on to the State Meet, it was clear that if I didn't win the City Championship, I'd be considered a failure – a promise never kept – a disappointment. I guess the fear was weighing heavily on me that day. I couldn't stop vomiting.

It was true that my times hadn't improved. I always ran only to win – not for time. My strategy was generally to just pull in behind the early leader – watch and wait – just sit back see how the race would unfold – and then take off only for the last half-lap. Sometimes I'd wait all the way to the final stretch before I started the real running. If the second-place guy ran 4:43, I'd run 4:42. If the second-place guy ran 4:24, I'd run 4:23. If he only ran 4:57, I'd only run 4:56. And that's how it went all year.

I was still racing and winning; I just wasn't setting records anymore. I honestly didn't feel like going out and killing myself trying to get a better time – winning was enough. But compared to the high expectations and all the Olympic predictions I had generated earlier, I seemed – in the eyes of many – to be coming up short.

I had an excuse.

I was doing it for the team.

That's a good excuse – right?

I was the one guy on the team consistently able to win three individual events, and garner enough points to make a difference in the team-point-total in the meets. So I was always saving myself for the next race. The first event was always the mile; the last individual event was the two-mile; and right in the middle was the half-mile. I always ran all three (plus often, one leg of the mile-relay as well), because the team needed the points. So I would only run fast enough to win and be ready for the next race. That satisfied me just fine. It was easy. I didn't have to hurt myself and it kept the coaches happy. But it didn't stop the newspapers from saying that I hadn't lived up to expectations.

So the City Championships became the day I had to prove them all wrong. And I felt like total shit. Seriously. I was sick about it. I wasn't even sure I was going to be able to get around the oval four times. It was that bad.

But the starter called us, so we lined up. Carl Meininger from Clackamas was the biggest threat. I tucked in behind him after the gun. He had a team-mate that pulled up on my shoulder and stayed there. They were obviously watching me as well.

The first lap was slow – thankfully – because I seriously wasn't ready to run. But when we came across at 67-seconds, everybody recognized that it was *way* too slow, so Carl Meininger picked up the pace. I had no choice; I had to go with him.

That's when it got bad. I wanted to throw up again right there on the second backstretch. I seriously considered stepping off the track and conceding. My demise seemed imminent. The predictions were coming true. Every part of me wanted to give up. But it was just too embarrassing with so many people in the stands to give up too soon, so I decided to try to make it to the half-way point.

We hit the half-mile at 2:07, which was still off-pace, but Carl had put in a hard 60-second lap and it hurt. It hurt bad. I was in hell.

I almost stepped off the track at the 880 mark. I wanted to. But I guess the faster lap must have hurt Carl too, because as we started into the first turn on lap three, I felt him slow up a bit. I guess that's why I continued into the turn. I was in serious difficulty. I just wanted it all to end. But when I sensed him slow, I thought there might – just maybe – still be an ever-so-slight chance of surviving. I told myself: "Just get through this lap and then decide whether to quit or not."

That backstretch on lap three was the most painful experience of my life. Period. Bar none. No exceptions. I never want to go through anything like that again. Ever. I don't know how – or why – I kept putting one foot in front of the other. I actually thought I was going to die. Every part of my body was screaming at me to stop running. I was totally ready to concede. It wasn't worth keeping up the charade anymore. I prepared myself for the inevitable humiliation and embarrassment. The newspapers were right. I was a failure.

As we hit the half-way point of the second turn of lap-three, just as we were moving toward the home-stretch before the bell, the grandstands came into view.

I looked up, for what I thought would be the very last time at all the faces.

But when I saw them, I realized that they didn't know.

They didn't know!

They were still cheering. And shouting. And watching. They were riveted to every step. They didn't know how badly I was suffering.

They didn't know it was already over. They were anticipating a final lap with all the excitement of a real athletic contest. They thought it was still a race.

What a crazy idea!

Just that simple, insane idea – that there was a whole other way to view this experience was all it took.

And that's when it happened. Clairvoyance! Total, absolute, crystal-clear clairvoyance! A switch got flipped somewhere in the Universe and I was granted the ability to know the future. I suddenly, effortlessly, and unmistakably knew the outcome. And nobody there that day was more surprised than I was. I was going to win. I didn't think it. Or hope for it. Or merely want it – I knew it! It wasn't about desire. Not at all. Desire had nothing to do with it. I knew I was going to win. There was no doubt. None. There was no fear. There was no pain. And most importantly, there was nothing – absolutely nothing – anybody could do about it. I saw the future. I was going to win.

I was so happy with my sudden revelation that I completely relaxed.

Incredibly, I ran wide out into lanes four and five and waved at the crowd. I left the inside lanes and ran by the grandstands smiling and waving up at the spectators like I was celebrating a victory lap while there was still an entire lap – another four-hundred-and-forty yards left to race.

Meanwhile Carl Meininger and Scott Johnson surged into the lead. The bell for the final lap sounded and I followed them – totally unconcerned – into the first turn of the last lap.

I was floating now. I didn't hear the timekeeper over the ringing of the bell as we started that turn, but it didn't matter. Nothing mattered. I actually felt sorry for Carl. He was running so hard and now there was nothing anybody could do to help him. Not even me. I was going to win and I had no control over it. I had seen the future. It was predetermined and impossible to change.

As I floated on down that last backstretch enjoying my newfound knowledge, I realized, somewhat to my surprise – that I was still several steps back and in third place, so I figured – since I was going to win – I'd better go ahead at some point and start my victory kick. So I took off. Just that easy.

When I got to Carl's shoulder though, as we headed into the final turn, he took off too. Poor guy. He obviously wasn't privy to the premonition. He was still fighting. He started his sprint.

I didn't care. It didn't matter. I already knew the outcome. I was all set. I didn't have a worry in the world. If Carl wanted to run hard and fight against fate, that was his business. It had nothing to do with me. I was fine with it. I just nonchalantly pulled in behind him again and waited for the home stretch.

We came out of the turn. Carl charged for home. The crowd was standing and cheering and screaming. I figured it was only fair to give them a good show. So I pulled up next to Carl for a few seconds to heighten the drama. I turned toward the stands and waved one last time at the roaring crowd and ran away from him to break the tape.

It wasn't my fault. There was nothing anybody could have done to change the outcome.

Now some will say that it was just my mind playing tricks on me about seeing the future that day. They will argue that my grand delusion became nothing more than a self-fulfilling prophecy. And they're probably right. But I promise that's not what it felt like. I've never been so clear about anything in my life. I don't know how I saw the future that day, but it sure made the race a whole hell-of-a-lot easier. And a whole hell-of-a-lot more fun, too.

But it never happened again.

I never saw the future again after that day.

And I never won another race.

That part of my life was over.

The part of me that made me special just wasn't enough anymore.

But I didn't know it, yet.

I was seventeen.

Kah-Nee-Ta
(June 1971)

"When can I get the money for Kah-Nee-Ta?" Mila was not usually so demanding.

"Remind me about Kah-Nee-Ta," I pretended.

"Oh come on," she laughed, "Kah-Nee-Ta! The morning after graduation! Warm Springs! Party! The whole gang is going! An entire week! You and me! Sex! Naked! Our own room! All to ourselves! Making love day and night! For an entire week!"

"Doesn't ring a bell," I teased.

"Laying by the pool? Lounging in the spa? All the booze you can drink? Did I mention sex? With me? Just you and me? Making love! You know! You! Inside me! All night long! You know this! We're going? Right?"

"Sounds kind'a over-rated," I was really pushing my luck.

Mila slugged me in the arm. "You don't want to sleep with me naked in a real bed for an entire week?"

"Well, I guess, I suppose I could do that," I grinned.

She slugged me again. But harder. Then she played her trump card: "Oh really? You don't want to spend some quality time with these?" She pulled her top up over her head and offered her bra-less breasts to me right there in the front seat.

I quickly glanced around the parking lot to see if anyone was watching and then helped myself to a handful of one breast and a mouthful of the other.

Just as I was really starting to feel ready, she pulled back, lowered her skimpy cotton top back down almost in place and got stern. "I'm serious. The Lodge at Kah-Nee-Ta wants the deposit by next week."

She wasn't playing around, anymore. She was worried I hadn't saved up enough money and she knew I couldn't ask my parents for it.

"I'll have the money," I stared at nipples poking through thin cotton. "We have two shows this weekend. Friday night is a Church dance in Hillsboro. I'll get $150. Then Saturday is at the D-Street Corral."

"How much is that?" She pressed.

"We get the door and it's usually at least $100-each. Don't worry." I reached over and traced the outline of one of her nipples with my finger. "Don't worry. I'll have it. You're coming to the show Saturday night? Right?"

"I'll be there." She pushed my hand away and scooted back to let me know I wasn't going to get lucky in the car again this afternoon, but she finished it off with a promise. "I want to make sure you don't blow all your money and miss out on the best week of your entire life."

She did come to the show that next Saturday night. And I did get the money. And graduation did, finally roll around.

There was all the usual pomp and there were speeches about rites of passage and the future and all that stuff about what a great accomplishment graduating was, but I honestly – seriously – got the feeling that it was just another day on the calendar – one that was bound to come around as long as you just waded through all of the other days in front of it. It simply felt, to me, like just another number on the calendar.

There was one problem with my particular calendar though – an ominous, gigantic, unfortunate, serious problem: the first night of my fantasy graduation week with Mila in Kah-Nee-Ta was a Saturday. And Ken Barclay, who was still our reluctant agent, had scheduled a show for the band that night. A big show. And he was being a dick about it.

"You don't understand," I tried to reason with him, "I already paid for the room and Mila is not going accept this. We gotta cancel that show. Or reschedule it. Or something."

"No possible way," Ken seemed angry lately, "it took me months to set this up. My reputation's on the line here. This is a Bill Graham showcase. Bill Graham himself is going to be there. You'll destroy everything we've worked for if you don't show up. Don't do this to me. This is a real opportunity for you guys. Don't blow it. It's what you said you always wanted. You *do* want it, right?"

"Of course I want it," I tried again, "but can't it be on any other night. This just totally sucks, man. I can't believe this is happening."

I took it to the guys. They were unanimous. They wanted to play the showcase. They reasoned that I could still fuck Mila all the other nights, so missing out on the first night shouldn't be that big of a deal.

Mila was not so understanding.

I tried to explain to her how important the gig was. Then I tried to talk her into coming to the show, so we could drive up to Kah-Nee-Ta together afterwards.

But she wasn't having it.

"The whole gang's going up. I'll get a ride with Karla and Ted." She was resolute. She was not going to miss out on any of the fun for my sake. "Our room is paid for. I'll check in. I'll see you sometime Sunday. Whenever you get there."

So our fantasy week didn't start off exactly as I had imagined.

I was worried about Mila being up at Kah-Nee-Ta without me. It bothered me that she was so ready and willing to go on ahead without me. It was all I could think about that whole day of the showcase.

I was still nervous at showtime. We didn't go on until after midnight. We played four originals and two covers. We played the best we could. I never did see Bill Graham, but they said he was there. As soon as we hit the last chord, I threw my gear into the trunk of my car as fast as I could. I dropped it all off at Roger's house and was headed east on Highway 26 toward Kah-Nee-Ta by 2:10AM.

I drove fast and got there just before 4:00 in the morning.

I knocked.

I knocked again.

I checked the number on the door. It was 2B. That's right. I knocked again. I took one quick, anxious circuit of the hallways to see if anybody else was up and awake after the first night of partying, but I couldn't stir a soul. I went back to 2B. I knocked a little louder.

Mila came to the door.

I was so relieved and happy to see her. I took her in my arms.

She embraced me one last time, stepped out into the hallway, and quietly closed the door behind her.

Then she uttered the words I will never forget:

"Somebody's going to tell you, so it might as well be me. I, umm, ... well, ... I slept with Larry Singleton last night."

That was the moment all the best parts of me died.

I knew right then I would never be the same.

"But... What about ...?..." I reached out to find the wall to steady myself.

"You're not the only one who gets to have a life. I get to have a life, too," was her explanation.

And it was her only explanation.

She stepped back inside the room that I had paid for and closed – and locked – the door behind her.

I slumped down to the floor in the hallway and sat with my duffle bag in my lap.

"No. No. No. No. No."

Two hours later, Timmy Tucker emerged from one of the rooms down the hall. I jumped up, ran at him, hit him in the face, knocked him down, kept running straight on out to my car, and drove back to Portland.

(I'm not sure why I hit Timmy. I certainly never had anything against him. To be sure, I was in pain, but there was something more to it than that. My best guess is that it was the humiliation. I think I was embarrassed that Timmy – and probably everybody else – knew about Mila and Larry before I did. And I just couldn't live with that.)

By 8:17AM, I was banging on Roger's door.

"Give me my guitars. I'm leaving."

"What?" Roger peered out from under his eyelids.

"I'm leaving." I glared. "Give me my shit. I'm out of here."

"Dude, after you left last night," Roger followed me to his garage, "we all got to meet Bill Graham. He totally dug us, man. He said you had charisma. Do you hear me? He liked us!"

"Doesn't matter." I couldn't even think about it. "I can't stay here. I'm going."

"What? Why? What are you talking about."

"No choice, man," I couldn't begin to explain it, "I just gotta go."

"Where?" Roger was beginning to perceive that I was in some kind of crisis. "Where you gonna go?"

"Don't know. Just gotta go." I hadn't even thought about it. "Anywhere but here."

"What about the band?"

"I quit."

Roger didn't understand.

Neither did I.

I left Roger. My best friend. Standing in his dad's driveway.

At 8:42AM I pulled into the driveway of my parents house on Oatfield Road where I had first laid eyes on the lovely bikini-clad mirage next door. I went straight upstairs to my room and started packing.

My mother sensed something was amiss and stepped into my room.

"I thought you were spending this week camping with your friends," she looked me up and down trying to assess the nature of the trouble.

"Yeah, well, that didn't exactly work out," I searched through my bottom drawer for my Bleeding Madras Shirt from the fifth grade.

"What's going on?" She already knew.

"I can't explain it, Mom."

"Try," she urged as she held her breath.

"I'm going."

"Going where?"

"Just going."

She didn't argue.

Not one word.

She could see I was leaving and that there was nothing she could say or do to stop me. I honestly don't know if she wanted to stop me, or not. She simply stood quietly in the doorway and watched me get ready to set out.

Before I took the last bag out to my car, I asked my mother to hold on to my treasure chest for me. She said she would.

That was my mistake.

I quickly took an inventory of my treasure chest one last time. I made sure my Beatles ticket was safe. I took a last glance at my *Most Outstanding* and *Most Valuable* certificates for track and cross-country. I found my ceremonial gavel with Student Body President engraved on it and tucked it safely into a corner of the chest. I sifted through the blue ribbons and birthday cards and love letters and trophies and I stumbled across an envelope with my Zig Ziglar list of "Five Goals for Graduation" stuffed inside.

I had to look at it twice.

I was taken aback. I couldn't believe my eyes. It was the list of goals I had written down when I was fourteen. I had forgotten all about it.

Without knowing it – without any memory or realization of it whatsoever – I had actually pulled off every single one of the items on the list.

They had all come true.

I blinked and shook my head and read the list again:

"Before I graduate, I want to:

    1) Go steady with the most popular girl in school

    2) Be Student Body President

    3) Own a Gibson Les Paul Gold Top guitar

    4) Write a song and make a record and hear it on the radio

    5) Be the lead guitarist in a big rock band and play a big rock show on a big rock stage in a big rock city where all the girls scream and clap and go crazy for me."

It was amazing to me to realize that I had never even noticed that my dreams had all come true.

It was even more amazing to realize that not a single one of my dreams mattered.

At all.

By 8:42AM the following morning, I was half-way to Los Angeles.

The Time Machine is Out of Order
(Summer 1971)

Maybe if we could violate the Second Law of Thermodynamics and put our consequences ahead of our causes, everything would be different.

Maybe I should have given myself more than two months to make it big in LA.

Maybe I should have found a cheaper place to stay than right on the boardwalk in Venice Beach.

Maybe I shouldn't have squandered what little money I had on cartons of deli-macaroni-salad and cases of Michelob.

Maybe I should have tried to get a job.

Maybe I should have had a better plan. Or any plan at all.

Maybe I should have known that nobody in Los Angeles would care that I had been Student Body President or that I used to be in a band.

Maybe I should have realized that nobody would be impressed that I used to go steady with the most beautiful girl in the school and was still pining over her memory, or that I could still outrun most high school boys.

Maybe when I could no longer pay the rent, I shouldn't have sold my backup guitar for gas money so I could drive out to Utah to stay with Twinkie. But that's what I did. Remember Twinkie? He was our very-first drummer. He moved away during that summer of '69 when I was fifteen. His family moved to Spanish Fork, Utah, which was where he was living when I called him and asked for a place to stay.

Maybe I should have anticipated that things would be different from when we were kids. But I didn't. I was unprepared for how much The Twink had changed. All of eighteen now, he didn't want to be called *Twinkie* anymore. Everybody in Spanish Fork called him Dennis, which was disappointing to me, since that was his name. But what I found really sad about the The Twink was that all of the ShitButtAssBiteHellFuck was all gone right out of him. He had turned into a fine upstanding full-fledged Mormon boy preparing to go on a mission for The Church of Jesus Christ of Latter Day Saints.

Maybe it would have been better if he had sent me on my way. But he didn't. Even though it was clear to both of us that we were different now, he was kind and gracious. He took me in. He got me a job throwing heavy bales of alfalfa up onto flatbed trucks in the hot summer sun in the hayfields of central Utah. It was hard, nasty, filthy work and the crusty old Utah farmers expected me to do it all day long. Those fat old Mormon landowners that paid me less then minimum wage for my labors – because they could – never missed a chance to say something to me (and to each other, while I could hear them) about my long hair, which I had allowed to grow over my ears. And for some reason, they seemed especially threatened by my mustache, because I had allowed it to grow around the corners of my mouth in defiance of Mormon conventions. I hated their rules and I hated them and I hated the hay.

Maybe my biggest mistake was calling my dad for help from Spanish Fork, because Spanish Fork is just down a short stretch of highway from Provo and BYU, where I still had a scholarship waiting for me. I had been accepted many months before and wrote to say I was coming, but never intended to actually show up. I was planning, if I went to college at all, to attend the University of Oregon instead (where I also had accepted scholarship offers). But I never told BYU, so fatally, my slot was still open.

Maybe it would have ended differently if I'd had the presence of mind to call my dad from Eugene, where I not only had a much-more-attractive scholarship offer waiting for me, but I also had a bid to live in a frat house on campus. (It was the frat that many of the Oregon track athletes belonged to.) Maybe I wouldn't have needed to rebel so much. Maybe I would have grown up a bit and become serious about my running. Maybe Steve Prefontaine and I would have become teammates and trained together. Maybe I'd have gone to the Olympics after all. Maybe.

And finally. Maybe if I'd have had the strength of character to refuse when my dad offered to pay for my housing and food and other expenses – but only if I went to BYU – not to Oregon. (He was convinced that being surrounded by non-Mormons was the source of all my wayward ways.) Maybe it all would have turned out differently. Maybe I wouldn't have spent so many subsequent years wondering how much better it might have been – what I might have accomplished – if I'd only had the balls to say "No!" to my dad.

Maybe if I had only stood up for myself.

But I didn't.

And that's the thing about time travel: it reverses the consequences and causes. It violates the Second Law of Thermodynamics.

Twinners

(Summer 1971)

The summer of '71 was my summer of choices. I had to choose between BYU and Oregon. I had to choose between the Mormon Church and the truth. I had to choose between Laura and Linda.

The problem was that I couldn't tell them apart.

Laura and Linda were identical twins. I met them my first day in Spanish Fork.

"Hey! You wanna go for a ride?" The Twink asked.

"Sure. What's there to do in this town?"

"C'mon, let's go."

The Twink and I hopped in his VW bug, flipped a U-ie on 200 South, turned right at the corner and started north on Main Street in Spanish Fork, Utah. Dennis (as he was called in that time and place) drove the seven blocks through town and when we got to the last gas station before the onramp to the freeway, he flipped another U-ie and headed back south down Main Street. I thought he'd forgotten something back at the house and we were going back to retrieve it.

But when we got back down to 200 South, instead of turning left toward his house, he flipped another U-ie and headed back north on Main Street again.

"What are you doing?" I asked.

"What do you mean?

"Where are we going?" I clarified.

"Here," was The Twink's reply.

"I don't get it," I confessed.

"Get what?"

"You're driving in circles."

"Oh! It's what we do here in Spanish Fork."

"Why?"

"Watch!" The Twink checked his rear-view mirror, pulled his car over into the right lane and slowed to just a couple miles per hour. As he did, the car behind us pulled up alongside and a teenage girl stuck her head out of the passenger side window of the other car.

"Who's your friend?" She half-laughed, half-shouted at The Twink.

"He's from Oregon. Gonna start The-Y in the fall." The Twink hollered back.

"Maybe," I corrected him. "Maybe I'm gonna go to BYU."

"You wanna meet him?" The Twink ignored me and shouted back to the girl.

She pulled her head back inside and rolled up her window. Both cars slowed to a stop. The front and back passenger side doors of the other car both opened and two identical teenage girls stepped out into the street. They ran giggling across in front of The Twink's headlights and came around to my side of the bug.

"Well, let 'em in," The Twink encouraged me.

So I scrunched forward and opened my door and pulled my seatback forward so the girls could hop into the back of The Twink's little bug.

Once they were in, I turned around to check them out. They were the same. They were dressed the same and had the same brown hair and the same brown eyes and the same brown eyebrows. Their names were Laura and Linda and I couldn't tell them apart. The Twink said that nobody in town could tell them apart.

They laughed and chattered and talked about people and things and places that I didn't have any clue about or understand at all. They still had a year of high school left and were enjoying the summer before it would be their turn to rule Spanish Fork High. Meanwhile, The Twink flipped another U-ie and then another and then another. I didn't quite understand this ritual, but I kind'a liked it. The more I watched and listened to the twins, the more it grew on me.

After several more circuits, we finally pulled into the Dairy Queen back at the corner of Main and 200 South and we ordered french fries and four Cherry Cokes. When they brought out the fries, there was no ketchup. They served them with cups of mayonnaise, instead. That was weird at first, but I learned to like that too. (I still like my fries that way, today.)

Over that summer, we found Laura and Linda on Main Street several nights a week. The Twink and I took to dragging Main in my '56 Chevy, because it was such a classic cruiser and it got us way more attention than his little VW bug did. It was also roomier in both the front and the back. Our pattern was that we'd find the twins somewhere on Main Street and they would invariably join us. The Twink would crawl back into my back seat with one of the twins and the other one would sit up front with me.

I never knew which one was with me and which one was with him. That was part of the fun. I always had to ask them who was who and which was which – every time. I tried many times over those summer nights to study their faces for any sign of demarcation

– any little telltale freckle or mole or dimple – but their secret was safe and we never knew for sure whether they were switching back and forth and playing games with us or just pretending to. And this went on most of the summer.

Until late one warm August evening, I pulled into the Dairy Queen with Linda – she said she was Linda – seated next to me. The Twink and Laura climbed out of the back to order our Cherry Cokes and left Linda and I to a rare moment alone.

As we waited, she did something neither her nor her sister had ever done before – she reached over and put her hand on my thigh – up high on my thigh.

A little startled by this unusual move, I looked carefully into her eyes and studied to see if she meant to do it on purpose.

She did.

"Careful there," I grinned, "you don't wanna start something you can't finish." It was a cheesy take-away move I'd learned from Roger back in the day. I'd seen him use it many times after our shows and it worked every time.

It worked this time too.

"Try me," Linda challenged. I think it was Linda.

I popped my Chevy in reverse and peeled out backwards leaving Laura and The Twink sitting on a red picnic table in front of the Dairy Queen. Linda shoved her right hand down my pants and I drove west on South 200 Street until it ended at the baseball fields. While she unbuckled my belt, I pulled into the back of the parking gravel and selected a spot where I could see in all directions. Before I could get the gearshift into park, Linda had my zipper down and my blood up.

"Let's get in the back," I slipped my jeans down out of the way.

She took the wad of gum out her mouth and placed it on the dashboard. She slithered over the back of the front seat and got ready to go in the back seat.

"Take off your top. I want to see you." I was going for the full experience.

She did and we did and it was indeed the full experience right there in the back seat.

I kissed her when it was over and thanked her and drove us back to the Dairy Queen, where Laura and The Twink were still sitting on that same red picnic table.

"Where did you two disappear to?" It was Laura that stepped over to my driver's side window.

And just exactly at that moment, before I could even lie to her, I noticed something – something that came as a genuine surprise to me. I looked at Laura as she stood outside my window at the Dairy Queen and couldn't believe my eyes. She wasn't as pretty as her sister.

Seriously. Linda was the prettier one. Linda, in fact, was beautiful and Laura was rather plain-looking. I could tell them apart from that moment on. It was easy. I didn't even need to see them together in order to tell. Linda was the pretty one. Laura was plain.

When I told the Twink about my epiphany and the reason for it behind the ball fields, he didn't react the way I expected him to.

"That's so wrong," he shook his head in disgust. "I should never have introduced you. What have you done?"

"I did what any guy would do. I thought you'd be happy for me." I was a bit startled.

"You thought I'd be happy that you committed fornication and ruined a good girl?" The Twink was turning into Dennis and not being nice about it at all.

"I really don't think I *'ruined'* anybody." I was quite taken aback.

"You're ruining your chance for salvation – and hers." Dennis insulted my intelligence.

"Oh you don't really believe all that nonsense, do you?" I thought we were more on a similar wavelength than we apparently were.

"It's not nonsense." Dennis stood his ground.

"Of course it's nonsense. Non-sense in the sense that it doesn't make any sense!" I explained.

"You believe it too," Dennis proposed. "Don't tell me you don't"

"No Twink, I don't know what I believe," I tried to be reasonable. "But I don't believe the stories about the ark and the flood and the whale and the tower and the garden and the snake and the apple and all of that. They're clearly just stories. They're not even good stories. They seriously couldn't even possibly be true. But I do believe there's something. Something that's pulling me back again and again and won't let me go. Maybe it's just guilt. I don't know."

"You ought'a feel guilty," Dennis wasn't going to play nice. "And that thing you're feeling is the Holy Ghost telling you that you're sinning ... and to stop it."

"I don't know Dennis," I almost laughed. "I admit that maybe I haven't cut the emotional string that ties me to the Church. Maybe I still want to please my parents? Maybe I'm afraid I might be wrong? Maybe it's nothing more than the fact that I've been told all my life that the worst, most vile, most unforgivable thing any person could ever do is question the Church? I don't know. I seriously honestly don't know what's got such an irrational hold on me. But the Joseph Smith Story? Come on! Golden plates? Kolob? Scrolls that are supposed to be from ".. The hand of Abraham .." that are actually common prayer books only a few hundred years old. And the whole off-again-on-again-polygamy thing? And the blatant racism? I mean, it's 1971 and anyone with '*Negro blood*' in their veins *still* can't hold the Priesthood or go to the Temple.   And how about how Native Americans are supposed to turn '*white and delightsome*' when they convert to Mormonism, because God cursed them with dark skin? Seriously? I mean, seriously? Really Dennis? You have to be a very special kind of gullible to actually believe all of this nonsense."

"I believe it." Dennis testified. "I believe it all."

"No you don't," I argued. "I don't believe you do believe it."

"Try me." Dennis challenged.

"Okay, I got one for you," I decided to take him up on his offer.

"Go," he didn't look worried.

"You're eighteen years old. You just became an Elder and were ordained into the Melchizedek Priesthood. Correct?"

"Yes! That's correct!" Dennis agreed with me so far.

"And as part of that, you now have the power to heal. You can lay your hands on people's heads and command them to be healed. Right?"

"Yes, that's also true." Dennis fell right into my trap.

"But when your little brother broke his arm last week, you drove him straight to the hospital. I saw you do it. You didn't try to heal his broken arm. You didn't even stop to say a prayer. You took him directly to the doctor. Because deep down where you don't want to look, you know it's all bullshit." I rested my case.

"That's not what those powers are for," he said it almost under his breath.

"Then what good are they?" I wasn't ready to let him off so easily.

"Sometimes, God has a plan." Dennis tried to wriggle out of it.

"If God has a plan – and it's going to happen anyway – because if it didn't, he wouldn't be God – then your Priesthood and your powers are completely irrelevant and unnecessary – and that goes for your precious prayers, too!"

Dennis just shook his head. He didn't answer. I didn't expect him to. Dennis was never going to be honest about the Mormon Church and both of us knew it.

"Hey man," I let him off the hook, "I don't want to argue with you about this, let's go drag Main Street. I mean that's what life is really all about anyway? Right? Just driving around in circles searching for something you're probably never going to find anyway? Right?"

"Okay," Dennis agreed that driving around in circles was better than talking in circles. "Let's go drag Main. But tonight, I'm not letting you and Linda out of my sight."

"Betchya I can tell the difference between 'em!"

I drove my point home one last time.

Just because I could.

The End of The Twink
(Summer 1971)

I watched the Lottery on black-and-white television with The Twink (I still called him that whenever we were alone). He got hold of his family's spare portable black-and-white TV and plugged it in right there in the privacy of his bedroom. We sat together on the edge of his bed and watched the Lottery.

It's not every day your life gets decided on national live television.

Gray-haired men in gray suits placed 365 numbered balls in one carousel and 365 balls with months and days in another. They started the carousels spinning and began dishing out life and death.

They'd pull out a birthday, then they'd select the numbered ball which determined the order the boys born on that day would be taken in the draft.

Dennis (the former "Twinkie" and later "The Twink") was born on August 3rd, 1953. He got number 3. He had to go to Vietnam. I got number 228. I didn't.

What do you say at a time like that?

Sometimes People Get In Your Face
(Fall 1971)

BYU was much more like the big time than I thought it would be. For some reason, I had the notion that I could easily go from big fish at Putnam High School to big fish at BYU. I thought that would be the natural progression of things. I was wrong. I was a seventeen-year-old small fish. A very small fish.

Although it was safely tucked away in the Mormon mountains, there were many more world-class athletes and authors and entertainers at BYU than I imagined. Before school even started, the first person I saw when I checked in at the athletic complex was Robert Redford – fresh from Butch Cassidy and the Sundance Kid. He was far more famous than even Steve Prefontaine. (The coaches used to drive us up to Redford's place at Sundance and we'd start at his house and run with his St. Bernard up the mountain.) And within weeks of registering, I found myself making a record album in the Osmond's recording studio and state-of-the-art television production facility in Orem.

My time at Brigham Young University was a big time education alright. But not the way anybody – not my parents – not myself – nor anybody else – expected. Or intended.

It all started with my Intro to Geology class. I couldn't believe it. On the very first day, the professor – a tenured BYU professor with a PhD – described the age of the earth as four billion (with a B) years old. Right there in public, in the daytime, where everybody could see and hear, he started right in on the fossil record and the overwhelming evidence for evolution. I found this absolutely shocking. My Father had always told me that evolution was a liberal, Godless hoax. Every Mormon I knew at the time claimed that the earth was less than 6,000 years old. I was very surprised to learn that they were tolerating science at BYU.

Even more enlightening was Intro to Anthropology. When early on, a student raised her hand in class and asked the Professor about using the Book of Mormon as a guide for locating archeological sites in the Americas, the Professor explained it this way:

"The Book of Mormon is a spiritual guide. Anthropology looks for physical scientific evidence."

"But," the student insisted, "the Smithsonian Institute uses the Book of Mormon to search for lost cities in South America."

I'll never forget his answer. It was simple. And powerful. He replied:

"No, actually, they don't."

Wow! I grew up being told the Smithsonian did that too.

What was going on here at BYU?

Track practice was much, much more personally enlightening. There were many world-renowned athletes at BYU in those days, including a living, breathing, walking-around World-Record-Holder (Ralph Mann) and a future Olympian and World-Record Holder (the other Freshman miler besides myself, Paul Cummings) and future Super Bowl Champions (Gordon Gravelle: Pittsburgh Steelers IX and X; and Golden Richards: Dallas Cowboys XII). Golden Richards caught touchdown passes in both of the Super Bowls he played in. I used to sit naked in the hot tub with Golden Richards and shoot spit wads with him at the ceiling in the steam room. But the big BYU eye-opener – the one that I remember most – was that the locker next to mine in the Athletic Complex belonged to Bennie Smith – the very first ever black athlete to play football at BYU. Bennie sort'a stuck out like ... well ... a black football player at BYU.

Because of the proximity of our lockers and his unusual social circumstances, I struck up a friendship with Bennie. In the first few minutes of us talking, I realized that I was almost eighteen years old and I had never had a single meaningful interaction with a person of color in my life. I had met people of other races before of course, but rarely, and mostly at our gigs – and always in passing. I'd never had more than a surface conversation with anybody who wasn't pretty darn white. (Yes, that's right, that's exactly how one-dimensionally monochromatic my upbringing had been. We thought we were the good white people at our house, because we didn't use the n-word the way most of our friends did.)

My relationship with Bennie might have been very brief and superficial as well, if not for his patience and understanding. He took a liking to me, but only after he got to know me – certainly not at first. We began with a decidedly troublesome first step. I asked him why he had accepted a scholarship to BYU, when the Mormon church didn't allow colored people in the Temple.

Bennie slammed his shoulder pads to the floor in frustration.

"Do I look *'colored'* to you?"

"What?" I realized I had angered him.

"Do? I? Look?" He repeated slowly, like I was a four-year-old. "*'Colored?'* To you?"

"No?" I stammered. "I'm sorry. I didn't mean anything."

"That shit pisses me off." Bennie glared at me.

"What am I supposed to say? Tell me what to say?" I pleaded, hoping against hope that he wasn't about to kick my ass.

"I'm a black man," Bennie informed me. "I'm a man. And I'm black."

"Got it." I swallowed.

The next few moments of silence were very difficult.

"Sorry," I finally stammered. "It'll never happen again," I promised. And it didn't. Even though he played football and I ran track, we became friends from then on. Pretty good friends, I thought. In the locker room, anyway. We didn't eat dinner together or hang out at each other's apartments or anything like that, but it was a baby-step. An important one for me. For one thing, I never used the word *colored* in reference to a human being ever again.

My uncomfortable, but eye-opening experience with Bennie made a real difference in the rest of my life. It served as a constant reminder to carefully examine my own thinking for my own biases – the unexpected, embarrassing, and ubiquitous, artifacts of my upbringing. But quite honestly, the Bennie-debacle wasn't the BYU epiphany that made the biggest difference in my life.

My biggest eye-opener, by far, that first Semester was my Religion class. Every student at BYU – even the non-Mormons like Bennie – were required to take a Religion class every semester. No exceptions. I was assigned to a section taught by the venerated and celebrated author, Eldin Ricks. He had written *The Combination Reference* and the *Thorough Concordance of the LDS Standard Works* – two of the most influential reference books on Mormon scriptures (both were books we owned and used in Church and Seminary often). Eldin Ricks was a leading authority on the subject of Mormon doctrine and was a Member of the First Council of the Seventy (high-ups in the Mormon church). I couldn't believe he was teaching at BYU.

He began his lecture one morning explaining the Mormon doctrine that Jesus was the God of the Old Testament. Mormons believe that Jesus and God-the-Father are separate beings. Mormons believe that God and Jesus are one-in-purpose, but that they are distinct, physically different personages – individual members of a Godhead.

"When the Old Testament refers to God," Elder Eldin Ricks began, "that reference is to Jesus Christ, the Son, and not to Elohim, the Father."

Suddenly a simple innocent question occurred to me, so naturally, and innocently, I raised my hand.

"Yes," he called on me.

"Well, Joseph Smith said: 'As man is, God once was; and as God is, man may become.'"

"Yes, go on," Elder Ricks allowed me.

"And since God is an exalted person with a physical body," I continued.

"Yes, yes ..." He waited for my question.

"Well, since the Church teaches that the purpose of coming to Earth is to gain a body, because a physical body is required in order to become a God, and ... well ... if Jesus is the God of the Old Testament, then ... well ... Jesus didn't have his body yet. He hadn't been born. Why didn't Jesus have to come to Earth and have a body before He became a God?"

I had never actually thought about it that way before. It just occurred to me on the spot, so I asked.

Unexpectedly, And in a much, much more menacing way than Bennie Smith ever did, Eldin Ricks got physically in my face. He placed his nose about an inch from my nose. He violently positioned his extended index finger up to the side of my head. And angrily spit the following words at me:

"DON'T! YOU! EVER! ASK! A QUESTION LIKE THAT AGAIN! AS LONG AS YOU LIVE!"

Word-for-word, that was his answer.

And he was the Church's leading authority on the subject.

I felt bad. I wasn't trying to be a smart-ass or a trouble-maker. It was just an innocent observation.

But I didn't ask any more questions in Religion class.

Ever.

Sex, Drugs and Public Relations
in the Rocky Mountain West
(Fall 1971 - Spring 1972)

The first time I ever smoked pot was at BYU and I didn't feel any effects at all. Evidently that's a common experience. Not the BYU part – the "not feeling anything the first time" part. My friend Gary Knox showed me how to inhale and how to hold it in, but nothing really happened.

I met Gary my first week at BYU. He was the bass player for a group called *The Free Spirits*. They were big, big stars in Provo, because they had appeared on the Ed Sullivan Show the winter before and were scheduled for a repeat performance the upcoming season. They were a group of extremely attractive, show-stopping, wholesome-looking singers – five guys and five girls backed up by a four-piece band (like those popular at the time on mainstream television, modeled after the Mike Curb Congregation). I didn't exactly relish the goody-goody vibe they projected, but they did seem to be the cool kids on campus. Plus, I'd read about the upcoming Ed Sullivan Show appearance in the school paper, so when I saw a notice on a bulletin board that they were holding try-outs for a new singer, I recognized my opportunity to follow in the footsteps of John, Paul, George and Ringo. Here was my chance to be on The Ed Sullivan Show. All hopeful and excited, I ratcheted up my best foot forward, signed up for the audition and sang *The Letter* by the Boxtops with all my heart. I intentionally sang it three half-steps too high to give it more energy. Gary Knox was the one who told me I got the gig. He also introduced me to marijuana.

~

The second time I smoked pot was also at BYU. But the second time, I couldn't stop laughing. I couldn't stop laughing and I also couldn't stop falling down. I would stand up just so I could fall down again. It was hilarious. Gary Knox told me that was normal, too.

I don't know why Gary and the other members of the rhythm section in The Free Spirits folded me into their secret society so easily. Perhaps they could see I was searching. The other singers in the group (five guys and five girls) all had squeaky-clean, Lawrence-Welk-ish, straight-laced, All-American appearances. And I guess with my new regulation BYU haircut, I did too – on the outside. But there must have been something in me that the rhythm section recognized, because we started smoking grass in Gary's dorm room after every rehearsal. It separated us few dangerous, cool individuals from the 30,000 wide-eyed Mormon kids on campus.

~

My first threesome was at BYU. The two girls in The Free Spirits who were undeniably the top two reasons for the group's popularity and success were Stella and Charlene. They were by far the most attractive and talented girls in the group and they were best friends. They lived together in an off-campus apartment.

Reason #1 – no argument at all – was Stella. Up close she had rather severe facial features – an almost square jaw and protruding cheek bones and big lips and big teeth and big eyes and big bleached-blonde hair. But from a few steps away? Or even better – from the audience when she was on stage – Stella was a sight to behold. She was the only girl I ever met in my life who had the body of a Barbie doll – an actual Barbie doll. She was two-thirds legs. She had the longest slimmest legs anyone had ever seen and they went all the way up to impossibly slender hips and a perfectly flat tummy. To make it even more unfair, Stella was blessed with seriously large, round anti-gravity tits that were difficult to ignore from any distance. And from far away, even her sharp facial characteristics made her appear just that much more striking. She was the star of the show at every performance. Oh yeah, and she could sing. She could really sing.

She was a born performer.

Reason #2 was Charlene. She wasn't as drop-dead stunning as Stella, but she was much prettier up close – softer and rounder and sweeter – still very much a beauty. She was the Marianne to Stella's Ginger. In fact, that's what we all called them – Ginger and Marianne – because they not only lived together and were best friends, they seemed to do everything together and to always have each other's backs. Together they ruled The Free Spirits and were more responsible for the groups acclaim than everybody else in the group put together.

Which was why I was so excited when they invited me over – just me – to their apartment one Sunday evening. I had a vague feeling that something was up (maybe one of them liked me?). I could only hope. Maybe it was something else entirely. When I got to the door, Stella pulled me in and offered me a martini, which was shocking to me at the time, because good Mormon girls don't drink alcohol or offer it to boys in their apartments. I had never had a martini before, or even seen one in real life, but I happily accepted her offer and thought to myself that maybe these girls weren't as straight as their public persona advertised.

And Boy! Howdy! Did that turn out to be the case!

Before I finished that first cocktail, which made me uncomfortable, because I didn't exactly know how to drink it, or how to hold it, or what it was supposed to taste like, Stella sat me down on the sofa between herself and Charlene and said: "Maybe you can settle an argument between us."

"Sure, if I can," I wondered.

"We can't decide which one of us gets to do this, first." And she leaned in and kissed me. I was surprised but I kissed her back. It seemed like the polite thing to do. After a moment, she pulled back, smiled knowingly, took my head softly in both her hands and oh-so-gently turned my face to Charlene. Then Charlene kissed me. Then she kissed me some more. Then Stella. Then Charlene again. I was totally unprepared for anything like this, but it was happening, and even though I was disoriented and confused, I liked it.

When Stella went for my belt, I jumped. I didn't mean to. It was just an involuntary reaction. Even with all the kissing, it hadn't occurred to me that this was going to go any further. But now it became clear that it was.

"It's okay, just relax," Charlene stroked my face for a moment and then kissed me harder.

Those first few moments with my tongue in Charlene's mouth and my dick in Stella's mouth were ... what? Incredible? Unexpected? Overwhelming? Indescribable? I'd say it was a dream come true, except that it wasn't. I had never dreamt anything like it – no nothing ever anything remotely like this. (They say a threesome with two girls is a common fantasy for all young men, but it never was for me. I honestly had never had that particular desire at all.) But here it was, happening anyway. Uncontrollable tingling began sweeping over me. The tingles started in the back of my head and cascaded all the way down to where Charlene and Stella were now licking and sucking and giggling and staring longingly into each other's eyes and kissing each other while they wriggled out of their clothes. I seriously didn't know what to do. I had never been so aroused in my life. I tried my very best to get on top of the overwhelming physical sensations and tried to collect my thoughts and hoped I could keep from embarrassing myself.

Then I began to worry. It sure looked like we were about to have sex. All three of us. How was that going to work? How was I going to satisfy both of these girls? One at a time, I guessed? Should I give them equal time? *Could* I give them equal time? Should we switch around? How and when do we switch around? Can I pick a favorite? I decided I liked Charlene better. Stella had the better body, but Charlene's was beautiful too, and Charlene's face was fresher and much more innocent-looking. But Stella sure was being awfully nice to me at the moment. I really didn't want to hurt either of their feelings. What if somehow, without meaning to, I accidentally let on that fucking one of them was more exciting than fucking the other one? I didn't want to do that.

I performed the best I could and lasted longer than I thought I would – thankfully – and after going in and out of Stella for a while, I eventually came inside Charlene, because it just felt so good that I couldn't help it. The girls laughed and kept right on kissing each other and I didn't know how to make a martini, so I helped myself to some vodka right out of the bottle and watched.

The next night was one of the recording sessions for *Flower Children* – our new Free Spirits album of popular cover songs. We cut the vocal tracks in the Osmond's recording studio in Orem. They let us use Marie Osmond's dressing room and I stole her toothpaste, because I had just that day squeezed the last bit out of my own tube. Gary stole Marie's bra, because he thought it was funny. The producer picked me to sing the lead on *He Ain't Heavy, He's My Brother*, and Stella sang *One Tin Soldier*. We did take after take that night and every time Charlene or Stella caught my eye, I grinned like an idiot. I couldn't help it. I was sure that the afterglow of our illicit tryst was obvious to everyone. But over the course of retake, after retake, after retake, it became apparent that we had gotten away with it. We were back to being wholesome All-American, Mormon kids.

Stella and Charlene had secrets. And now I was in on one of them. That was almost as fun as our night together.

~

My second threesome was also at BYU. But I liked the next one even better. It was Thanksgiving 1971. I remember, because it was the night before we left on our big USO Tour. I had Thanksgiving dinner with the Twink's family in Spanish Fork and then drove back to Provo as soon as I could get away. Stella had asked me over after turkey and I assumed Charlene would be there too. I hoped so anyway. But when I arrived, Charlene wasn't there. Charlene was out on a straight-date with one of her return-missionary boyfriends (or so I was told). Instead, Kevin was there. Kevin was the keyboard player in The Free Spirits. He was also one of my after-practice-pot-smoking insider buddies.

Stella handed me a 35mm camera and asked if I would take some photos of her. I looked at Kevin. He looked at me. We shrugged. I said, "sure."

Stella could be seriously alluring when she wanted to be. She definitely knew how to get a guy all worked up. Before long, her clothes were on the floor and she was sucking Kevin's cock. When they moved to the bed and he went inside her, she motioned for me to come over and get my dick out too. It was pretty damn exciting.

The best part was that this time I didn't have to worry about satisfying anyone but myself. Stella was being taken care of just fine. I simply let go and allowed myself to experience the sensation of it all. I really liked it. We took turns and changed positions in every way we could think of and had a great time. It was fun. The three of us fucked all night long.

There was one point in the festivities, when Stella was on her back sucking Kevin off and I was repeatedly driving inside her with my hands on both her hips to keep her from flying off and out of position, that something interesting happened. Stella reached down and took my right hand and started pulling on it. I let her take it, because I thought she was going to place my hand on one of her fabulous breasts, so I thought, "sure I can do that for you." But she kept pulling my hand up past her breasts to her face and I suddenly realized that her intent was to put my hand on Kevin's cock. My completely unconscious, yet powerful and immediate aversion to such an idea – and the quickness and force with which I involuntarily yanked my hand away – made it clear that such a thing was not going to happen – ever. But I found it interesting. It didn't bother me one tiny bit to be naked and to be having sex with Kevin – as long as there was girl in between us. It wasn't my fault. I guess I was just born that way. Good to know.

~

My first orgy was at BYU. (Well, okay, it wasn't exactly on campus, but it was with the BYU kids, so that counts.) The morning after the threesome with Kevin and Stella, The Free Spirits gathered at the Salt Lake City airport to embark on our USO Tour. As soon as he was able to get the guys in the rhythm section off away from everybody else, Kevin announced, right there on the concourse, that he and I had had sex the night before. But the way he told the story, he left Stella out. He thought that was funny. I was embarrassed and was about to protest, but quickly thought better of it, because I didn't want to blow Stella's cover – or my chances for a return engagement. And also because I figured if I protested too much, everybody would think I was gay, anyway. So since I didn't really know how to respond, I simply let Kevin get away with it.

I sat next to Charlene on the plane. She said she'd heard all about mine and Kevin's night with Stella and said she was sorry she'd missed it. She promised to get her revenge before the tour was over. That gave me a boner just thinking about it. She played with it a little when we were sure nobody was watching and she got me pretty riled up, but we were careful and that was as far as we dared go on the airplane.

Our first stop was Miami, but instead of putting us up in a hotel, like the rest of the tour, we stayed that first night in a Miami area Stake Center (Stake Centers are like regional headquarters for Mormon Wards). Local church-members provided us with sleeping bags and pillows and all the *pot luck* we could eat and we bunked down after that first performance right on the stage in the cultural hall.

When the lights went out, the whispers started. I learned that Kevin had let slip the real details to Gary (our bass player) and to Rodney (our drummer) and that they wanted in on any future adventures with the girls. Incredibly, Kevin had spoken to Stella about it during the flight. I thought Stella would be pissed. But she wasn't. Not even a little. In fact, she had gone ahead and recruited Valerie to join in the fun.

We all (four guys and three girls) snuck back into one of the carpeted meeting rooms in the Stake Center and nobody bothered to watch the door. Stella got it started. With Kevin again. She pulled down his pants and went to work on his dick while the rest of us stood around nervously watching in the dark. Then as our eyes adjusted, Stella turned and knelt on one of the upholstered chairs and Kevin entered her from behind. It was strange and dangerous and crazy and thrilling. Soon they were thrusting away and Charlene got naked and started touching herself. Gary finally worked it up and jumped at Charlene, and she let him, so I held back a bit and noticed that Valerie was a still a little reluctant. She was interested and aroused (I could tell by her hand inside her pajama bottoms), but it was clear that she wasn't as comfortable as the other girls just yet. I decided this was my chance. I moved over to her before Rodney could work up his courage.

I liked Valerie. She wasn't as pretty in the face as Charlene, or as overtly sexual as Stella, but she was tiny and tender and vulnerable and just my type. She didn't have much in the way of breasts but her tummy and hips and butt and legs and that delicious skin that covered her entire naked body as I helped her out of her pajamas made me almost forget where I was.

When I got down on one knee and started to lick between her legs, she hesitated and almost pushed me away. I was afraid she was going to change her mind, so I took her by the hand and we stepped out of the back door of the room and found ourselves, completely by accident, in the baptismal font.

She let me fuck her right there in the waterless baptismal font and it was the certainly the most outrageous – but only the second-most memorable – experience of the night. When I was done, we stepped back, still naked, into the other room where Charlene and Stella were feeding Gary's cum to each other and I watched while Valerie let Kevin and Rodney both fuck her on the carpet.

That's the truly memorable part that stayed with me in the days that followed. I replayed the memory of it over and over in my mind. And it came as a real surprise to me that it affected me the way it did. As I watched Valerie pleasuring first Kevin, then Rodney, then both together, I felt myself beginning to fall in love with her a little. "Good girl," I said to myself as I watched her overcome her reluctance and her inhibitions. She let herself go and in doing so, she pleasured not just the guys, but also herself. It got good to her. She seemed to be in absolute ecstasy. I thought she never looked more beautiful.

Our second show was at Guantanamo Bay, Cuba. It wasn't a prison then; it was a U.S. military base. They flew us over in a big Army cargo plane with no seats, just benches. It was colder than I thought it should be on the way over and I was tired from two nights in-a-row of no sleep. But we got through the performance and the GIs all went absolutely crazy for the girls in the group (if they only knew). We hoped they would let us stay overnight in Cuba, but the Commanding Officer wouldn't allow it (something about safety). So when we found out that we would have to fly back out the same day, Valerie and I snuck into the latrine at one of the empty barracks and I had her real quick again while she held the door closed with her feet and I looked out through the barbed wire window and satisfied myself.

On the way back to the mainland, we all complained that CBS had canceled The Ed Sullivan Show, because this was the week we were supposed to be on. I was particularly miffed, because that was the whole reason I'd joined the group in the first place. I probably would have made a bigger stink about it if I hadn't had Valerie to sneak off with for the rest of the Tour. Since there was no Ed Sullivan Show, we had a free date in New York City. I took Valerie to a fancy restaurant and spent way too much money. Then we took a New York City cab ride (which was a dream come true for me) and finally a carriage ride through Central Park. The carriage driver covered us a with a blanket and Valerie put her head on my shoulder and held me close the whole time and it felt really, really good.

The rest of the tour was a bunch of military bases in West Germany and Italy, as far as I can remember. Which were all the same. It wasn't like actually getting to experience Europe and it wasn't anything close to the big rock tour that I had hoped for, but the audiences were boisterous and enthusiastic. And that's always fun. At every base, there was always a GI or two eager to share his pot with us. The only two things I seriously didn't like was that after every show, they required us to go out and do a reception line, signing autographs and selling albums. We moved stacks and stacks of 12" vinyl records on that tour. They brought carton after carton out of the back and we had to stay as long as any GI wanted to fork over cash, meet the girls and buy our crappy record. And the lines were long – very long.

The other thing that made me crazy for the rest of the tour was that I never got another chance at Stella after our orgy night. Stella and Rodney somehow connected that night and inexplicably, to everyone's utter bewilderment, the next morning they paired off and became a couple. And Rodney didn't want to share. Rodney was no fun at all.

~

The first time I dropped acid was when we got back to BYU. We couldn't find anybody to sell us pot one weekend. The whole State of Utah had gone dry it seemed. There was no marijuana to be found. But all the dealers had LSD. And we wanted to get high. The dealer that sold us the acid said to be careful, because the last guy took off all his clothes and ran around campus naked claiming to be Jesus.

"Cool. Give me one." I was willing to try it.

It was pure Window Pane LSD-225. I touched a transparent tab the size of a small freckle to my tongue and didn't know if I had actually got any on me or not until about a half-hour later.

Woah!

I decided acid was God.

It wasn't just better than sex, it was an eight-hour orgasm. And it was more. Much, much more. Infinity finally made perfect sense – it was suddenly so obvious. Religion melted away. Philosophy was child's play. The meaning of existence was obvious and absolutely understandable. If only there were words. But words were just things. Meaning was so much more than words. It was so simple. And powerful. And beautiful. And sexual. My black-and-white Easy Rider poster turned technicolor. Everything turned multidimensionally spectral and got wavy. The universe was warm and fuzzy and electric and Planet Earth was only one of an infinite number of possibilities and it all felt so fucking good. I stopped going to class. I stopped going to track practice. I stopped going anywhere that wasn't going to get me another hit of acid. I did LSD every day for more than a month after that first trip.

~

The first time I shot heroin was at BYU. One night, we couldn't get any acid. Even when we drove up to Salt Lake City in desperation, there just wasn't any. We eventually scored some heroin instead. And a kit. Gary knew what to do. As we drove back to Provo, Gary melted some brown smudge in tin foil with his lighter and held the surgical tubing for me. I plunged the needle in myself. It wasn't instantaneous. It took about a minute. At first it was a warm, pleasant sensation that swept over me and for a few moments, I enjoyed being the most relaxed I think I had ever been. I thought I was really going to like this heroin stuff. But another moment later my eyes began rolling back. My body got numb and went limp on me and I melted into the backseat.

Then I had to throw up. I remember somebody holding my head outside the window in the freezing cold mountain air and everybody being pissed because I made a mess in the back seat. I didn't care that they were pissed. The nausea was so bad that I just wanted to die. I wretched up all the way back to Provo and finally passed out from all the effort. When I woke up the next day, I decided I liked LSD better.

~

The first time I got arrested was at BYU. On campus, there were 30,000 Mormon white kids, two large black athletes on scholarship, and about nine of us who were actually living on the edge. As it turned out, we were also being way more obvious about it than we realized. That didn't ultimately matter though, because it also turned out that Charlene was a narc. I never saw her again after the State Police rolled up. They caught me with thirty hits of Window Pane LSD stashed in a .22 caliber shell casing. I don't know why I had it there, but they knew exactly where to look and they took me to the Provo City jail along with Kevin and Gary and some girl named Ellen who just happened to be along for the ride that night.

They had me for possession, sales and distribution. Class A narcotics. In Utah. In 1972. That's seven years for possession and up to life-in-prison for sales (I never sold a hit of anything to anyone, but the quantity I was caught with put me over the legal dividing-line between mere possession and sales). No matter how it gets cut, that's a long time inside the Utah State Penitentiary. I would have felt much worse about it, but I hadn't quite come all the way down from the previous night's high yet. That's when the Sheriff suddenly appeared, yanked me out of the cement cell and dragged me upstairs to a room where Dallin H. Oakes – the actual real-life President of Brigham Young University – was waiting for me.

Evidently, The Church of Jesus Christ of Latter Day Saints is deadly serious about their public relations. Dallin H. Oakes – future Justice of the Utah Supreme Court – explained to me in measured and not uncertain terms that BYU did not have a drug problem on campus. There was no illegal drug activity at BYU and there wasn't going to be any. Additionally, since BYU was, at that time, embroiled in a growing national controversy (many colleges were beginning to boycott BYU sporting events, protesting the Church's policy of not allowing blacks into the Priesthood), my irresponsible actions could have further jeopardized the University's standing in the court of public opinion.

Dallin H. Oakes – future prospect under both Gerald Ford and Ronald Reagan for nomination to the Supreme Court of the United States – was there to protect the reputation and public image of the University and the Church. The fact that I was still technically on the BYU track team (I had stopped going to workouts, but that was beside the point as far as the newspapers would be concerned) and the fact that I was in The Free Spirits – the highest profile entertainment group on campus – made my situation especially troubling for the BYU Administration. Dallin H. Oakes – future Member of the Twelve Apostles of the Church of Jesus Christ of Latter Day Saints – determined he was not going to allow my selfish behavior to cast a negative light on the University or the community or the Church.

The deal President Oakes offered me was that I leave school – that day – that very day – and never return – ever – and that as long as I didn't disclose anything to the press – even if they asked – as long as I just said "no comment" – there would be no record of my arrest – anywhere.

Dallin H. Oakes had the power to make that happen.

I took the deal. And nobody ever asked.

I had dodged a bullet.

I owe my freedom – my ability to come and go – even the very flavor and fabric of the rest of my days – to a rank cover-up – to institutional Mormon dishonesty. My life would most definitely have headed down a decidedly different track in the Utah State Penitentiary, if the Mormon General Authorities hadn't been so keen on manipulating their public image.

And by extension – mine.

Thanks Guys.

Hot Sox Knox & the Mudsharks
(April 1972)

Getting arrested scared the shit out of me. Not at first. Not until the next day. And even then, it wasn't the legal jeopardy or the fear of going to jail that frightened me – that part never seemed real – it was the idea that I had been found out – uncovered – exposed. That was the terrible part. I felt like a fraud – laid bare.

I'd been kicked out of school. My locker at the athletic facility had been cleaned out. My run with The Free Spirits was over. But honestly, none of that mattered all that much. The problem was that I was no longer fooling anyone. I felt naked. I needed to run for cover. But where? And how?

Valerie picked me up from jail and she was completely freaked out. The first thing we figured out was "no more drugs." She made me promise. "No more drugs. Period." So I promised. And I meant it. I never ever wanted to be that exposed, again. Beyond that, I had no plan at all. The only thing I could think of was to see what Kevin and Gary were going to do about their similar situations.

We landed a few days later, Gary, Kevin and I, in Boulder, Colorado. Kevin's parents lived in Denver and they arranged to let us stay in their summer house just outside of Boulder. (In the spring of 1972, Boulder, Colorado was a phenomenally poor choice of location for youngsters trying to stay away from drugs.) Oblivious, we moved into our new band house and it occurred to us that this was our chance to make our dreams come true. All we needed was a drummer. We made a pact. No drugs. Gary and Kevin said grass didn't count and they continued to smoke pot, but I didn't. I had promised Valerie. And I meant it.

Not being high all the time since the first day we had met, I immediately noticed something amazing about my friends that I hadn't before. Kevin and Gary were both seriously gifted musicians. Always before, in all my previous bands, my band-mates had been chosen on the basis of proximity and friendship. They were mates first and band-mates later. This time, it was the other way around. These two guys were actually talented – very talented. I should have recognized that if Kevin had landed the gig as the keyboard player for The Free Spirits at BYU where practically every one of the 30,000 students grew up with piano lessons, he must have been rather outstanding. And he was. If he had ever heard a song, he could play it – with either hand – and nail it the first time. His ear was that great. Kevin's talent for even the most intricate harmonies was stellar and his vocal range seemed to have no top end. He was seriously amazing.

Gary was no slouch either. He could play more than twenty different instruments – all by ear – or by notation – or both. He had an understanding of the complexities of music that I hadn't even glimpsed. And for some reason, he shared that gift with me. Gary Knox taught me music theory over the next few months. He made music so simple and beautiful and understandable. I will always be grateful to him for that. After years and years of toiling through endless music lessons, Gary unveiled for me the straightforward mathematical relationships between the scales and chords and keys and he totally flipped the switch on for me. What a difference!

We put an advertisement in the Boulder Daily Camera to audition drummers and after a few painful false starts, found a seriously hard-hitting stick-wizard by the name of Quincy Mack. We called him Mack. And we were ready. We began rehearsing for hours on end – days at a time. The empty bottles started to pile up. The band house soon smelled like stale beer and marijuana. Those were good days.

Between us, we had a collection of well over a thousand records (of course there were duplicates), but we only played two albums that whole summer: The Who's *Who's Next* was our favorite, because it was just so iconic and powerful, and we also wore the vinyl thin on Frank Zappa and the Mothers of Invention *Live at the Fillmore East*.

We learned every nuance of every note on both sides of both records. We played them incessantly, both on the turntable and on our instruments. We got so we could copy them to a ridiculous degree. I focused and listened and studied and tried hard to capture Pete Townsend's power chords with the combination of my Les Paul and my Marshall Stack and endeavored to copy Frank Zappa's guitar solos note for note the best I could. Kevin and Gary had it down, though. In addition to his musical skills, Kevin was also an electronics whiz. He went to Radio Shack and got some oscillators and filters and transistors and got so he could duplicate the sounds of *Baba O'Riley* and *Won't Get Fooled Again* on his organ. Gary could both scream like Roger Daltry and deliver the high falsetto of Flo & Eddie on the Zappa recordings. We were ready to become stars.

All excited, the band name we were going to ride to stardom was *Hot Sox Knox and the Mudsharks*. Gary Knox had earned the nickname *Hot Sox Knox* back in his dorm his freshman year, because he would throw a portion of his dirty laundry into an empty dryer in order to reserve it while he washed his first load in the one of the washing machines on his floor. The funny part was that in order to keep people from removing his dirty placeholders, he would turn the dryer on. The problem of course came when the first load was done and he opened the dryer. Evidently the aroma of hot smelly dirty socks of the Gary Knox variety is an experience not to be envied. We thought *Hot Sox Knox and the Mudsharks* was the best band name ever and we were ready to rock and roll.

We started playing out, in Denver and its suburbs mostly, and audiences were generally confused and annoyed with our twenty-minute rendition of *The Mudshark Medley*, but they jumped up and down and got all excited every time we played *Bargain, Happy Together*, or *Behind Blue Eyes*. My favorites were *Tears Began To Fall* from the Zappa record and of course our big show-stopper medley that we ended every night with: *Born to Be Wild* which segued seamlessly into *Magic Carpet Ride* which then folded into Kevin's organ intro, Gary's scream, and the subsequent power and excitement of *Won't Get Fooled Again*.

(By the way, as a side-note: If you've never swung your arms wildly and blasted out those final chords of *Wont Get Fooled Again* with your Marshall Stack turned all the way up live on stage under the lights in a hot, crowded room full of excited, adoring music lovers, I highly recommend that you do, because it's just a fucking awesome thing to experience. And it never gets old.)

After the shows, the guys and I would sometimes bask in long, fanciful conversations about our hopes and dreams. A favorite topic was speculation about our future wives (it's funny to me now that we were still so conventional, in spite of ourselves). We also talked a lot about the meaning of life. Kevin was adamant that there was no meaning or purpose to anything. Gary generally argued that meaning was something we just make up as we go along. Mack used to like to say: "The meaning of life is that it ends." They all three sounded right to me, but it seemed that the ultimate logical conclusion to every argument – as far as the band was concerned – was always to find a reason to break out the weed. I was still trying to be good, so whenever the weed came out, I'd slip away as inconspicuously as I could. I was trying to keep my promise to Valerie.

Valerie used to say: "Tell me what you do and I'll tell you the meaning of your life." I missed her. But for some reason, I stopped writing to Valerie and started writing letters to Mila, instead. I was trying to recapture something from the past, I guess.

To my surprise, Mila started writing back. Mila said in her letters that we would always be special to each other. I loved that.

So I spent my nights playing in the band and my days writing letters to Mila and practicing my guitar. I often found myself, acoustic guitar in hand, up on my favorite rock in the forest above the band house in the middle of the night. I often played until the sun came up. In fact, I usually played until the sun came up. Those were my Rocky Mountain High days. My just-a-boy-and-his-guitar days. My free-to-be-me days. My still-trying-to-figure-things-out-but-happy-to-be-alive days. My happy days.

They didn't last long.

Playing Guitar is Not a Job
(June 1972)

Mila came to visit. She flew from Portland to Denver. I drove down from Boulder to pick her up. The plane was delayed and I got nervous waiting for her to land. When she finally walked casually up the ramp, it was almost midnight and I could tell that I was happier to see her than she was to see me. I even said something to her about it. She replied that the person doing the waiting was always more eager for the reunion. I wanted to believe that's all it was, so I let it go. Besides, she looked better than ever. I didn't want to blow it.

Driving back to Boulder up the dark, winding mountain roads, selectively chatting about some of the adventures we'd encountered during our year apart, it became apparent to me that I had changed much more than Mila had. It was really good to see her though. She looked and felt like home.

I was just getting ready to tell her that she felt like home, when something behind us smacked us hard and forced us over into the guard rail. We had just started out over a steel and concrete bridge and suddenly Mila's side of my car was screaming and scraping and grinding to a halt.

The driver of the car behind us had fallen asleep. Evidently, just a millisecond before he hit us, he awoke and tried to swerve left, but he clipped my left-rear fender and flipped his car over onto its roof.

As we scraped to a screeching halt against the retaining wall, the other car went spinning by like a top – up side down – right down the middle of the bridge and spun and spun until it finally slowed to a stop in front of us.

241

I did not want to get out of the car.

I looked over at Mila. She looked at me. We were okay. But I imagined blood and gore and mayhem in the upside-down hunk of metal resting silently and eerily just ahead of us. For some reason I pictured bunches of bloody babies inside. I did not want to get out and go see.

I most definitely didn't have the courage to go look. But my body went anyway. While my mind was still searching Mila's face and looking for a reason to stay right there with her, my body – by itself – on its own – without any volition on my part – got out of my car and ran over to the upside-down driver's side door of the other car.

There were no babies – just one guy inside. But he was an upside-down bloody mess. I panicked and tried to pull open his door, but it was crumpled shut. I tried his back door. Same thing. I felt useless. While I frantically tugged and pulled and got nowhere, he kicked out his passenger-side window and crawled out onto the highway.

He wasn't as hurt as he looked. He had only cut the bridge of his nose, but it was bleeding like a geyser. His face was bathed in blood. He pulled himself to his feet, looked at Mila (who by now was standing there in the road with him), and said: "You better go sit down, Miss." She *did* look like she was going to faint.

Mila pulled a clean t-shirt out of her suitcase and the other driver held it between his eyes to slow the bleeding while we waited for the tow-trucks. Gary picked us up from the tow-yard in the middle of the night. When we finally got back to the band house, Mila wanted to take a shower. I joined her. It was a wonderful reunion after all.

We took a lot of long, warm showers together that next week. Those showers were the last, best, cleanest part of us together. When the other driver's insurance company contacted us, they said that since my car was more than fifteen-years-old, the damage was too extensive to warrant a repair. They called it a total loss and offered me a check for the value of the car.

I should have argued. It was my '56 Chevy. The car I got for my sixteenth birthday. The car I was driving when I got my first ticket that very first day for "Driving while Embracing" with Mila. The car I drove to all my gigs. The car I drove on all our dates. The car Mila and I parked behind the drive-in in. The car we both lost our virginities in.

Yes, Mila was there for the first day and the last day of my '56 Chevy. I could have argued. I guess I could have even refused.

But I had my sights set on a used, in good-condition, Martin D-28 acoustic guitar I'd seen at Boulder Music and the check from the insurance company was just enough to pull it off. I knew I'd never have a better chance at a real Martin D-28.

"You need a car," Mila couldn't believe I was considered buying a guitar instead.

"But it's a Martin D-28." I tried to explain.

"You already have a guitar," she remembered our bout about my '53 Les Paul Goldtop.

"Not like this one," I tried again to reason with her.

"You can't drive a guitar to your precious gigs," Mila was flabbergasted.

"Gary has a car. And Kevin has a van." I was sure it would be fine.

"What about me?" Mila was beside herself.

"I can always borrow a car if I need to," I was willing to put up with the inconvenience. "You don't understand. I may not get a chance at a real Martin again for a long time."

"You may not get another chance at me again – ever," she

threatened.

"But I need it." In my heart, it was already a done deal.

"Besides," I added, "it's my job."

And then she said it:

"Playing guitar is not a job."

There it was.

It was finally the essential core of the same discussion we'd been having since she arrived. Mila wanted me to come back to Portland with her. She said we could get married. She had already found me a position at a hardware store in Milwaukie. Her step-uncle was holding a spot for me. She said I could get promotions and eventually we could buy a house and have some babies and things would be just like we always dreamed.

But that wasn't my dream. I loved Mila and I would always love her. And I told her so. But I was only just starting to find the courage to tell her that I didn't want to get a job and buy a house. I wanted to play guitar.

She already knew.

Gary drove us to the airport. I kissed her good-bye. She cried. I cried. On the way back up to Boulder, Gary and I figured out that someday we'd find girls who would let us be ourselves.

"I don't want a wife that's going to think she's allowed to have an opinion about where I go or what I do," I explained.

"Yeah, I don't want a wife like that either," Gary laughed.

Bullets and Brothers
(June 1972)

Gary complained of headaches often. He rationalized they were the reason he was so inclined to self-medication. I always thought he just liked getting high and that the headaches were a convenient excuse he had stumbled upon. But back in Utah, Gary's doctors had found a shadow on some of the images when they took X-rays of his brain, so one Monday morning, Gary had to drive down to Denver General Hospital for some further tests.

Kevin and I took advantage of the break and went for a hike in the canyon above the band house. We needed to get outside. With Gary gone for the day, we couldn't rehearse anyway, but the real reason we needed a break was that Kevin's older black-sheep brother Kurt had come up to Boulder on his Harley and had forced his way into our band house in a very unwelcome way.

Kevin's brother Kurt was unpleasant and unimpressed and unbearable. He promised he wouldn't stay long, but while he was there, he seriously cramped our style. He didn't buy that we were going to be famous musicians. And he said so. Often. He laid such a heavy stain of pessimism and negativity on our dreams that we didn't like to play, or do much of anything else, when he was around. We couldn't wait for him to leave. Kevin and I needed to get away for a while.

We trekked up as far onto the mountain as we thought we dared go in just our jeans and t-shirts. We pulled up a rock each and Kevin lit a joint. I declined his offer to share explaining that I was high enough already. I liked it up there. We stayed in the thin air basking in the altitude most of that afternoon, until the temperature began to drop. I didn't want to return, but for safety's sake, it was time to get back down the mountain.

We had just found the main trail when a bullet whizzed by only barely above our heads.

There's nothing else like the sound of a bullet piercing the air just inches from your skull. It's unmistakable. While we were looking at each other in amazement, trying to figure out what to do, we heard a shot and a second bullet. The second bullet, right at shoulder level, zipped directly between us.

We both hit the ground as flat as possible and started shouting as loud as we could for whoever it was to stop shooting at us. After a few moments of silence, we got up and ran on down the trail. A couple of twists and turns later, the sparse foliage gave way to open space and we saw some kids with a rifle running away below us.

"I'm going to kill them," I declared and started even faster down the path.

"No!" Kevin shouted. He stopped running and stood in the trail panting with his hands on his knees. "They've got a gun. You probably don't want to piss 'em off. It looks like they're tryin' to get away. We should let 'em."

We did.

All the way back down to the band house, I couldn't get the sound of the bullets out of my brain.

"I wonder what it's like to get shot," I confided to Kevin.

"We almost found out," Kevin replied. "I didn't like it."

"No," I clarified, "really shot, I mean. When David Summers came back from Vietnam, he had a Purple Heart. I remember I asked him what it was like to get shot. He said it felt like a bunch of bee stings. That's what he said: '... bee stings.'"

"Must have been a pretty small caliber, if they were only bee stings," Kevin reasoned.

"Yeah, small caliber," I thought, "that probably wouldn't be so bad."

I thought about it for another minute and actually said, "so when we get back to the house, I want you to shoot me."

Kevin laughed.

"I'm serious. Life is for experiencing things."

I was talking myself into it.

"You're not doing enough drugs," Kevin analyzed, "You're just tryin' find a way to stimulate yourself and keep your 'no drugs' promise. You're makin' yourself crazy."

"Maybe so, but I want to see what it's like." I was almost convinced.

"You're batshit crazy." Kevin refused at first, but by the time we reached the house I had talked both of us into it.

We took a heavy old army jacket we found in one of the closets and lined the back of it with the thickest science textbooks from Kevin's parents' library. Then we found a good-size piece of sheet metal in the attic and carefully placed it just right, so that it would hold the books in place.

We went out behind the house and I hunkered down on an old metal barrel that had been used for burning trash. By this time, Kevin's older biker brother Kurt, without being asked, had joined in the project. He went along with the idea just fine like there was nothing unusual about it at all. It was the first thing he hadn't objected to since he got there. Kurt helped Kevin situate the sheet metal and the textbooks and the army jacket just right. Then Kurt placed his motorcycle helmet on my head while Kevin loaded the .22

rifle and they measured off about fifty paces back into the woods.

I sat in silence. Waiting. I scrunched my shoulders forward to try to get them in front of the books and I pulled my neck down as close to my shoulders as I could manage. And waited.

The first shot hit me square in the middle of my back. (We later discovered the bullet had pierced the jacket, gone right through the books and put a healthy dent in the sheet metal.) I felt it hit me, but it didn't knock me over or anything.

"Hold still," Kevin shouted.

So I waited for another one.

The second shot whizzed an inch from my right ear with that very familiar bullet-in-flight-sound, but much, much louder and much, much closer and much, much scarier.

I hadn't considered the possibility of Kevin missing his mark. Until now.

I began to worry.

It suddenly dawned on me that maybe the motorcycle helmet wouldn't be up to the task of stopping a bullet. And now it seemed possible that maybe Kevin wasn't a very good shot.

I'd suddenly had quite enough of this experience.

I jolted and jumped away from the barrel and turned to wave off the third shot and couldn't believe what I saw.

Kevin and Kurt were fighting over the gun.

Seriously fighting over it.

They both had their hands on the rifle. They were pulling hard on each other and struggling over a loaded gun. Kurt was doing his best to wrestle the gun away. He wanted to shoot me too. And there were only seconds to spare. Kurt was surely going win the battle, but Kevin was holding on for dear life – mine.

I seriously had no idea Kurt was so eager to shoot me. I guess he didn't like me either. It occurred to me that if Kurt had shot me, it would have been my own fault.

And then something else occurred to me. Maybe Gary wasn't the only one who had something wrong with his brain.

Naked, Stoned and Stabbed
(July 1972)

Gary's favorite song was *Bargain* by The Who. He loved that song. He confided in me several times that his greatest fear was that he would "... drown an unsung man."

To be honest, I never could figure out why he liked that song so much. Don't get me wrong. I liked it too. Still do. But it's not as iconic as *Baba O'Riley* or *Won't Get Fooled Again*. I always thought *Bargain* was a love song about a guy who'd give anything to be with the girl of his dreams. But in all the time I knew him, I never knew Gary to have a girlfriend. He didn't seem to even want one. He liked sex enough. I was sure of that. He certainly enjoyed our BYU-Miami orgy and I watched him pick up girls after our Mudshark shows. But they were always just one-offs.

I asked him about it more than a few times. He always said the same thing: "One and one don't make two. One and one make one."

That didn't make sense to me. Especially coming from Gary – from someone else – maybe – but from Gary – I didn't see it.

Gary was logical. He usually saw things so clearly. He had deciphered the rules and shared them with me. He showed me how scales go together. He revealed to me the algorithmic relationships of sounds. He laid bare major and minor and diminished and augmented and he explained the numerical differences between jazz and blues and modes. Gary taught me the math behind the music.

Now it seemed he was going against everything he'd ever helped me with.

Now he was saying that math was irrelevant. Gary argued that *Bargain* was about eschewing the material world in exchange for enlightenment.

"I'd gladly lose me to find you," he'd say.

"Sounds like a love song to me." I still wanted to argue with him.

I was often tempted to point out the discrepancies in his world-view. But I remembered that Gary was my friend. And whether it made sense or not, he could have any favorite song he wanted.

Gary came back with his diagnosis from his doctor visit in Denver and said that he felt "... naked, stoned and stabbed."

I knew exactly what he meant.

I wanted to promise him that he wouldn't "... drown an unsung man," but I didn't.

I didn't know if such a promise could be kept. I didn't know what the future held. And I didn't know if Gary was ever going to be sung or not. So instead, I promised Gary that I would always be there for him. I thought I could, at least, do that for him. I sincerely hoped I could keep *that* promise.

Because, more and more as time went on, it was Gary that was always coming to my rescue. When I was searching, he was there. When I needed a friend, he was there. When I needed a fix, he was there. When I got busted and needed a place to stay, he was there. Even when I just needed a ride, because I'd traded my car for a guitar. Gary was there.

And I'd call that a Bargain.

"... The best I ever had."

Colorado Orange Sunshine
(July 1972)

In the wee morning hours of the 24th of July, 1972, Gary dutifully drove us back up the mountain from the very last Hot Sox Knox & the Mudsharks show. None of us had the slightest hint that it was all about to end. It was almost six in the morning by the time we got back to town.

If only we'd gone straight home.

"I know where we can get a first call," Gary suggested.

"I've heard of last call," I shouldn't have said anything, "but never 'first call.'"

"Same thing, but on the other side," Gary laughed, "Tom's Tavern starts serving at six. We can make it just in time."

So we did. We got there just as the bar opened. We belly'd up. It might have been because I'd been up all night. Or the several beers head-start I'd consumed in the car coming up the mountain. Or maybe it was the atmosphere in Tom's Tavern that morning. Or just my general state of mind. Or some other serious character flaw. But my resistance was low and my inhibitions were falling away fast.

So when Gary left the bar for a few minutes and returned with several hits of Orange Sunshine, I popped one.

"Careful man," Gary cautioned. "This isn't like that Window Pane Acid we used to do."

"How so?" I looked up from my beer.

"It's not as pure," he explained, "I hear it's got strychnine and arsenic and all sorts of shit in it."

"Sounds like a trip," I slurred.

"Yeah, it'll be a trip alright." Gary settled in for the ride.

Kevin reached over, selected an orange nugget about the size of a peppercorn and tossed it into his mouth. Mack took one too.

After a few more beers, Mack, Kevin and Gary all started tripping. They wiggled their fingers at each other and seemed amazed by the experience. They got far-away looks in their eyes and talked about how everything was starting to get all wavy on them.

"I don't feel anything," I complained. "Maybe mine didn't take. I must have got a dud."

"Just give it a minute," Gary was busy with his personal hallucinations.

"Gimme another hit," I told him, "that last one didn't do anything."

Gary didn't object, he pushed another orange peppercorn my direction.

I tossed it in my mouth and took another swig of beer.

As I put the beer down, the first tab kicked in. When I went to lower my mug, there were suddenly more than 360 degrees in a circle and the mug just kept falling down and down and down and it went through several cycles of several different dimensions before it finally came to rest on the bar.

Woah!

Then the bar started to swirl. The wood grains in the bartop began dancing around and weaving through and between one-another. I watched them dance for a while, and when they started flying up out of the bartop and into my face, I turned to Kevin to see if he could see the swirling flying woodgrains too. But when I looked over at Kevin, his face divided into three horizontal sections, waved goodbye for a few seconds and then melted away. Kevin became liquid cellophane and disappeared into an electric puddle on the floor.

I looked over to see if Gary was still with us. Gary hadn't shaved that day and his whiskers were dancing. It occurred to me that Gary's whiskers should be called "zinos." Gary's *zinos* began growing in and out of his face and swirling into long – very long – spinning tentacles that turned from black to blue to purple to red to orange and then back to blue and black again. Gary's eyebrows came down to meet his whiskers and they danced around while the rest of his face rippled and rolled. Gary's eyeballs looked intensely into mine like something bad was about to happen. And then Gary's face melted too.

I turned away and decided not to think about it.

"Don't even think about it!"

I was afraid thinking about it would make me crazy.

There was a nail in the wall behind the bar I hadn't noticed before. It began wiggling. It wriggled and twisted and oozed out of the wall and became three twisting nails and then seven swirling nails that waved and swayed and wriggled and refused to hold still.

That's when the walls started breathing. They came in. They went out. They swirled around. Nothing was solid anymore. The world was reordering itself right in front of my eyes. Solid became liquid. Then solid again. Time fell away. Time ceased to exist. There was no framework. No starting or stopping point. I began to think I should grab a hold of something. I reached out for something. Anything. But nothing was there. I looked down at the barstool I was sitting on. It was suspended in a heaving, moving, spinning swirl of forever and I suddenly couldn't sit there anymore.

I decided I needed a breath of fresh air. Something real. Something natural. Something pure. I summoned up the will to head for the door.

I got outside and the mountains began breathing the same way the walls had before. Trees were spinning and swirling and wiggling and leaving trails behind them as they spun. The mountain came up and got in my face. Then when I breathed out, my breath moved the mountain miles and miles away. But when I inhaled again, the mountain came rushing right back at me. It was going to absorb me. The mountain was going to overwhelm me.

"You can handle this," I said to myself.

"No, you can't handle this." It was a voice.

"Get it together," I told myself.

"Too late," the voice prophesied.

"You're strong," I told myself, "You can handle anything."

"You can't handle this." The voice was still there.

"Ignore the voice."

"You can't!"

"Get it together!"

"You'll never get it together. Ever again."

"C'mon! You can get on top of this this thing," I gathered my wits the best I could.

"You cannot get on top of this thing."

"You can do it. Keep it together. C'mon man, buck up," I garnered every bit my willpower.

"You can't do it. It's too big. It's bigger than you. You're fucked for sure this time."

I knew I was in for a fight. And the stakes were high. I was sure of that. I didn't know what the stakes were exactly, but they mattered – and they were forever. I had to find a way to survive. But how?

I looked around for something. The mountains were still breathing in and out and the trees were still swirling and throwing off colorful trails as they spun, but now the mountains and clouds and trees began turning electric and poisonous and plastic and liquid.

I needed something. I saw the words *Mila* and *Valerie* float by waving – not the people – not the faces – just the words. The letters were pink floating liquid cellophane. They had an electric charge and they were spelled M-I-L-A and V-A-L-E-R-I-E, but I didn't know what either word meant. In fact, I had no idea whether either word had any association with anything real at all. I only knew the floating plastic words were important, because they seemed to be all that was left in the world, so I reached for the words. But I couldn't get to them. The electric charge became too much to bear. I couldn't get hold of the words. The word G-A-R-Y went waving by. It was purple electric liquid cellophane. I didn't know what it meant either. It was just a word. But it was something. Something important. So I reached out for it. It crackled with electricity and became too hot and too dangerous to be near.

The mountain melted and the trees dissolved and the plastic floating electric words floated away and the Universe became an impossibly thin, single string and my entire life from birth to death became an infinitesimally small point on that string. It occurred to me that maybe the world isn't at all what we think it is. The string of the Universe was so infinitely long and my entire existence was so obviously inconsequential and immeasurably puny that I actually found comfort in it. My being, my selfhood, my very existence, my father's entire life, his father's life, everyone-I'd-ever-heard-of's entire life from Abraham Lincoln to Genghis Kahn was such a ridiculously small speck on the experience of the string of the Universe that none of us mattered. At all! Not even a little. None of us amounted to anything that could even be measured.

Time, even if time existed, which it didn't, didn't matter either; it wouldn't have meant anything, even if it did.

Then the voice came back.

"This is the part you won't remember," it told me.

"Which part?"

"Doesn't matter," the voice reiterated, "this is the part you won't remember."

I don't remember that part, but the next part that I do remember was the white hot electric liquid power source.

I tried to move towards it. But the closer I got, the more liquid and electric it got. It was white hot electric liquid death.

I reached for it.

I tried to get closer. It crackled with energy – too much energy. It pushed me away. The force was too strong. I tried and tried, but couldn't get to it. I was afraid of it. It was death. But it was all there was. There was nothing else. I was drawn to it.

I tried and tried, but I just couldn't get to it.

Something fuzzy and round came into my view and fell from the sky and it came together and formed the face of a nurse in Denver General Hospital and she was saying something to me and it was three days later and I didn't know where my guitars were.

Comeuppance
(1972 - 1973)

I have no memory of how I got to my parents' basement back in Portland. But there was a mattress down there. And I was on it. Brother number three – Layne – had been promoted to my former bedroom upstairs in my absence, so I was relegated, in my shame, to a corner of the basement. It was all I needed. I wasn't going anywhere.

Agoraphobia set in. I couldn't leave that mattress. I was afraid to go outside. Any little surprise or unexpected snippet of sound could trigger another panic attack. I couldn't go anywhere. Everything scared me.

Every little noise launched another flashback.

I couldn't trust my own brain.

My confidence was gone. I didn't know where it went or what had happened to it. All I knew was that all that confidence I used to have was gone. I didn't know if it would ever come back.

I knew I would never be the same. I could no longer say or do. Anything to anyone. I could no longer go. Anywhere. I could only sit and wait for the next flashback – the next time the world would stop making sense – disorder itself and fall apart. It scared the holy hell out of me.

It occurred to me that I wasn't sure what I was thinking. Or if I even could think. Flashbacks came and went and I didn't seem to have control of my own mind. And that bothered me. I just wanted to be able to think a thought. Seriously. Just one thought. That was my big idea. That's all I wanted. That's not much to ask.

But I couldn't do it. I figured I should be able to. But I just couldn't seem to pull it off. I thought I should try to reboot my brain by first thinking a thought. So I tried to force a thought into my head. But no thoughts came. I sat on my mattress for days on end trying as hard as I could to think a thought. But it just wasn't working. No matter how hard I tried, I couldn't formulate an idea. Of any kind. Nothing that I was sure of. All I knew was that I could no longer trust my own thinking.

So my parents got somebody to do my thinking for me. They brought the Bishop down to meet me on my mattress. I confessed everything.

The Bishop was far more fascinated by the sex than the drugs. I remember he was particularly interested in each moment of penile insertion. He wanted me to describe each event in great detail. It made me uncomfortable, but I revealed them to him, because he asked me to.

When we were done, the Bishop told me that if I could "… stay away from sex for a whole year…," then he'd see if the Mormon Church would still send me on a mission. He said my flashbacks would have to clear up, but that he'd see what he could do. I figured I wasn't going to be having any sex anyway. Even the idea of going outside – where the world might at any moment begin to re-order itself – was more than I could bear. No, I wasn't going to be leaving my mattress anytime soon.

Mila was still next door, but only for a few more weeks. She got a job as a teller in a bank in Westmoreland and she decided to get married to the manager of her branch. She came to see me once in the basement, but when I heard her coming, I didn't know what was happening, so I got scared and froze in fear right in front of her.

She didn't stay.

But after she left, my guitars were in the basement with me.

I picked up my Martin D-28.

I started to play. I played it for a year. Hours every day. Every day. It was everything to me. That guitar saved me. (A car certainly wouldn't have been of any use to me.)

The first sign that I was getting better was that a thought occurred to me.

The thought was this:

"Man, if the Mormon Church turns out not to be true, I'm going to be seriously pissed off about this year with no sex."

The second sign that I was getting better was that my parents decided it was time for me to get a job. I couldn't just sit in the basement and play my guitar forever. And they were right. It was time.

I answered an ad and endured an all-day series of tests with several hundred other applicants. I remembered that I liked tests. I'd always been good at tests. Tests were a chance to show off. These were mostly aptitude tests and critical thinking assessments as far as I could tell. There was also a manual dexterity test, which was new, but I could play piano with both hands and I was quite accomplished at scales with my left hand on guitar. (It wasn't until many years later that my Angel-of-Wonderful, the G-Dog, figured out that I'd probably been born left-handed, and was forced to be a righty, because I started school in the 1950s, but that's a different story.) In any case, I must have done pretty well on all the tests, because out of the hundreds of people who took them that day, they hired me.

And just in time too. My parents packed up the other nine kids and moved them back to Idaho. They didn't want the same things to befall them that had happened to me. They blamed the non-Mormon environment in Portland. They desperately wanted my brothers and sisters for find Mormon wives and Mormon husbands and the odds were increasingly against that in Oregon. So my father finally found the motivation to quit his job and went back to teaching. I moved into the spare bedroom at Ronny's parents' house on King Road and started my new job.

I loved that job. Seriously, I did. It was making gold teeth. My supervisor would bring me an articulated plaster cast of somebody's mouth after a dentist had prepped them for a crown or bridge and I would take a ball of wax and mold it into a tooth, or a series of teeth. When I got the wax model just right, we'd make an impression of my creation and pour molten gold into it and when it cooled down, we'd polish it up and send it back to the dentist.

It was fun making gold teeth. I liked it. But I didn't know why. What I didn't realize until years later, was that the great thing about that job was that everybody else who worked there had also passed all of those tests. Everybody was smart. Everybody was talented. Everybody was skilled. Everybody was cool. I liked them. There were some great people there. It was the best straight job I ever had. By far.

Then one day, she walked in. Every young man has an idea in the back of his mind what the ideal woman looks like. And she was mine. Absolute perfection. I won't try to described her except to say that she was my idea of divine. And I guess I'm not very original, because I wasn't the only one who noticed.

Nobody started work until she arrived. We all waited until she entered the room each morning. We watched in awe as she walked back to her station. We reveled in her presence. And only when she started in on her tasks, could we begin our daily routine. She was breathtaking.

Her name was Jenny Foster and she was out of my league. Hell, she was out of all our leagues. But just by being in the building, she made coming to work an absolute joy. Did I mention that I loved that job?

And wouldn't you know it? That's when my mission call came.

The Mormon church wanted to send me to Japan. I'd taken a language aptitude test at the Bishop's behest and I must have passed it. I was hoping for France, but I got Japan.

Suddenly, I no longer wanted to go. I didn't want to miss out on watching Jenny Foster coming to work. I was going to miss her so much. But because I couldn't even imagine any real future with Jenny Foster, I went ahead and put in my notice at work.

On my last day, even though I had only rarely spoken to her before, I walked back to Jenny's station to tell her I was leaving.

"Why?" She looked up at me. She was beautiful.

"A mission for the Mormon Church," I answered.

"Why?" She looked more puzzled than before.

"It's what I'm supposed to do," I tried to explain.

"Well, we can't let you go without a party, can we?" Jenny Foster's eyes lit up.

I got all excited. My stomach started doing flips. I rode with two of the guys from my station over to Jenny Foster's apartment as soon as we got off work that day. I couldn't wait to get there. I jumped out of the car and practically ran up to the front door. There was beer and wine, but I didn't drink any. There was grass and smoke and blow, but I didn't do any. The party was nominally for me, but I was far from the center of attention. Everybody was just excited to be invited over to Jenny Foster's apartment.

And it was a good time. The hours passed quickly. Great conversations. Great people. Best party ever. I didn't want it to end.

I didn't want to ever leave that party, but as midnight approached, I thought I probably should. My ride was taking off, so I went to find Jenny Foster to thank her and to say good-bye.

"Why don't you hang out for a bit?" She suggested, "I'd like to talk to you about this Mormon thing you're doing."

"I guess I can," I stammered, "if it's okay."

"Of course it's okay," she smiled at me again. "Hang out right where you are. Let me go clear everybody else out'a here."

So I waited while she made everyone else leave. I sat on her sofa and watched them go. When the last one closed the door, she came over to me, plopped down, spun around, laid her gorgeous head back on the arm of the sofa, and threw here long, lovely legs up over my lap.

I wanted to touch her leg, but I didn't dare.

"Oh, I'm glad that's over," she exhaled, "I've been trying to get you alone all night."

Nothing could have surprised me more.

I swallowed.

"Really?"

"Yes. Really." She leaned up and mussed-up my hair. "Do you want to take a bath with me?"

I froze. I didn't know what to say.

"Yes," came out of my mouth.

"Let's go," she jumped up, grabbed my hand and led me to the bathtub. She started the water running, poured in some bubble bath, lit a candle and turned off the lights. I could barely breathe as she slid out of her clothes and stood naked for me in the candlelight. She stepped into the bubbles and motioned for me to get in with her.

I stumbled over my belt and pants and socks and boxers and climbed as quickly as I could into the tub.

Jenny Foster touched me right there in the candlelight. She started with my shoulders, then my arms, then my chest. And she let me touch her. Her face. Her shoulders. Her neck. Her breasts. Jenny Foster was magical. We caressed each other in the bubbles. We kissed. She reached down for my dick. I tried to make it hard for her. It wasn't quite there. I focused on how incredibly beautiful she was. She stroked it. I wanted her more than anything else in the whole world.

It wasn't working.

She smiled, "it's okay, let's try something else."

She rose up out of the bubbles with her perfect body and stepped out of the tub. She handed me a towel and whispered, "Follow me."

She led me up the stairs to her bed. She laid me in all my wet nervousness down on her comforter and put her moist, warm, wonderful body up against me. I held her there. She held me there. I tried to get ready. She reached down to help me again.

I let her try.

She was good. She was patient. She was kind. And she kept at it.

But it wasn't working. I couldn't get hard. I didn't know why. No matter how I tried, I couldn't make it hard. The best, most exciting, most-dreamed-about adventure of my life was quickly devolving in to the worst, most humiliating real-life nightmare I had ever experienced.

("No! Not now! Not this! Please don't let this happen. No. Not to me. No. No. Not with Jenny Foster. No. Please. Anything but this. C'mon. C'mon. Get it up. Let's go. When you gonna get a chance like this ever again? It's now or never. Come on penis. Let's go. C'mon!")

"Just relax," Jenny Foster tried to comfort me, "it's okay, we can try again later."

(But I didn't want to try again later. I wanted her now. Right now. Oh please! Let me have her! This was so humiliating and so infuriating and so painful and so so so so so so unfair. Why me? Why now? Noooooooooooo!)

Jenny began drying herself off. She was incredible in her raw natural nakedness.

What kind of a man couldn't get hard for her?

I sat up on the cloud that was the edge of her bed.

Her room smelled heavenly. I wished I was dead. How would I ever live this down? I put my head in my hands.

"Don't worry about it," Jenny tried again to put me at ease, "stay the night. We can try again in the morning."

When I thought about what I had just missed out on, I wanted to die. I would have given anything – anything – to make it all right. Why couldn't I make it happen? Why? I just couldn't do it. And I didn't know why.

Jenny was great though. She was understanding and wonderful. She laid me back down on her pillow. She stroked my head and hair. She whispered for me to just relax and let myself go, so I finally fell back there on her covers like a useless, impotent lump of less-than-a-man until we eventually drifted off to sleep together.

When I woke up, my dick was hard. And Jenny Foster was sucking on it.

I was so happy.

I looked down to see if it was really happening.

And it was.

She had my cock in her mouth and her beautiful head was bobbing up and down on it. Her long luxurious hair was falling all over me and the head of my penis was alive and erect and basking in victorious ecstasy. This was the best thing that ever happened to me in my whole life. The back of my head started to tingle and roll. Oh it felt so good. So swellingly, throbbingly, incredibly good. I couldn't stop it. I spasmed and climaxed and came in her mouth. I let it all flow. A whole year's worth. Oh what a feeling!

Jenny Foster didn't swallow my cum though. She didn't spit it out either. She held it in her mouth. And with devilish smiles in both her eyes, she slowly brought her lovely cum-filled face up to mine. She kissed me; she was holding a year's worth of my jizz in her mouth. She was trying not to laugh. She tried to force my mouth open with her lips. I resisted. She insisted. I tried to turn my face away. She grabbed me by the ears and forced her lips to mine again. She began prying my lips open. I wriggled around. She held me down. I clenched my lips together. She placed a finger in each corner of my mouth and pulled hard. She put her mouth on mine and pushed with her tongue until I let her in. She dumped my entire load back into my own mouth. I gagged and spit it out over the side of the bed as she roared with laughter.

I fell in love with her. I stayed there all day and we made love again and again and again. I got my stuff out of Ronny's parents' house and moved in with her the next day. We lived together for the next year. She was twenty-one and I was nineteen. Jenny Foster taught me everything about sex. We did it in ways and places I'd never dreamed of. She even had books on all the different ways to do it. She especially liked it in her mouth and in her ass. I'd never done the ass thing before and sort'a figured I could be doing it to a guy, but she really liked it in every way possible, so we fucked and made love and wailed away and I learned a lot and had the time of my life.

I never came in her mouth again though.

Or anyone else's either, for that matter.

Human sexuality is such a strange, mysterious, complex jumble of nerve endings, mental images and unfathomable urges. Jenny Foster in all of her glory would suck on my dick for hours sometimes. She really tried to make me come again that way many times. And it always felt great. It was awesome in fact. But no matter how close I got to climax, I could never again let it go. I never came in another mouth.

It became my special quirk – my superpower.

I used it to my advantage time and time again over the coming years. I even used to announce my unique ability from the stage in the seedier clubs, when we were on the road, just to rustle up willing contestants.

More than a few women took it on as a personal challenge during those years on the road, but that's a whole other set of stories that we probably needn't bother with.

The Trial
(September 1973)

Six High Priests were seated on my right and served as my defense team. Six more High Priests were seated on my left and argued against me. The President and his two Councilors presided over the proceedings and delivered the verdict.

Everyone said the odds were in my favor. After all, my own father had, until recently, been a member of this very body. He had been one of them. It was extremely fortunate for me that he was still remembered and revered. In fact, without exception, every single one of the High Priests held my father in near mythic regard, since he sold his house in Portland and moved his remaining nine children back to Idaho in hopes of sparing them the fate of his eldest son.

So I had that going for me. I also had character witnesses, of course. And my side argued that the General Authorities of the Church had considered me fit and worthy enough to call me on a mission to Japan. Plus the fact that excommunication is rare – it's something the Church really doesn't like to do, if it can be avoided. It all added up to a very high likelihood of me getting off easy.

But then, there were the charges. The primary and most important charge was fornication. There were minor transgressions as well – disobedience, several incidents of past drug use, and a general pattern of worldly behavior. But the biggie was fornication.

I sat quietly through the proceedings and listened to the back and forth about the evils of sexual relations before marriage. Which iniquities required sanctions? Which warranted forgiveness? Over all, it seemed to be going pretty much as expected. I hadn't planned what I was going to say, but I was sure they would at least give me a chance to say something.

When it was my turn, I surprised them all – and I surprised myself – when I rose to my feet and stood before them:

"If any one of you knew what it's like to be with Jenny Foster, this trial wouldn't be happening. Sex with her is not a bad thing. It's good. I like it. I like it a lot. I intend to keep right on doing it. Sex isn't wrong. Nothing that feels so good can possibly be as bad as you're all making it out to be. And it doesn't matter that we're not married. If you think being inside Jenny Foster is evil, that only proves how messed up and stupid you are."

I sat down.

They excommunicated me.

It wasn't until I was alone in the men's room afterwards that I felt – and faced – the impact of what had just happened?

I couldn't believe it. The shackles were off. I was nineteen and for the very first time since nine-months-before-I-was-born, I was free. It was baptism in reverse.

Standing alone at the urinal, looking straight ahead at a blank slate of a wall, my first few minutes as a non-Mormon felt very, very strange indeed. My skin seemed different. I touched it. Yes, it felt different. Inside my skin. That was somehow different, too.

I moved over to the frosted men's room window, but couldn't see through it. There was light coming through the textured glass, but the rays were diffused, jumbled and distorted. I couldn't make out a clear image.

I cracked the glazed glass window open and peered out at the world.

And tried to imagine the possibilities.

The Magic Ticket – Episode Two
(September 1973)

When my mother learned of my excommunication, she was back in Idaho and overcome with grief.

I wasn't there, so I didn't witness it, but she must have suffered terribly, because she found my treasure chest (which I had foolishly left in her possession when I set out on my adventures), and she started going through it.

Then she started a fire.

One by one, she pulled out every photograph, every class picture, every birthday card, every report card, every love letter, every blue ribbon, every certificate and every award I had ever saved my entire life and threw them all into the fire.

When I heard from my sister what she had done, I was crestfallen.

My Beatles ticket was in that box.

I could carry on without all of those other things. It would have been nice to have the love letters, but I was confident there would be more. And the awards? ... Well, they'd have been nice to have, too.

But my Beatles Ticket?

I didn't even have to ask.

It was gone.

No matter how much I wished. No matter how much it hurt. No

matter how many times, or how many ways, I tried to work out how things might have turned out differently. There was no possible way in heaven or on earth to ever bring it back. There was nothing I – or anyone – could ever do about it. Some things can never be undone.

My Beatles ticket went out into the universe and no longer existed as a separate thing, except in my memories. No matter how much I longed for it, wished for it, or ached for it. It was no more.

And my childhood right along with it.

I certainly wasn't grown up yet, and likely wouldn't be for a very long time, but both my cherished magic ticket and my precious childhood were history. Never to be experienced again.

I hung up after getting the news from my sister, and immediately sensed that the world was disordering itself again. I felt a flashback coming on. I didn't know what to do. I needed something. But what? I needed to talk to Gary. Gary would understand. He saw things clearly. He saw through things. He knew the real me. He would understand. He would know what to do. I needed to talk to Gary. I didn't have his number, but I knew his dad's name and I knew he was from Concord, California. Gary's parents would know where he was. I called information and got the number.

Gary's Mother picked up the phone.

"Hi, I need to talk to Gary Knox. Is this his parents' number?" I asked.

"Who is this?"

"Gary used to call me 'Doc.' We played together in The Mudsharks," I hoped they would remember.

"Oh, honey, where are you?" She did remember me.

"I'm in Oregon and I really need to talk to Gary. Do you have a number for him?"

"Oh Sweetie, Gary doesn't have a number. He's gone."

"What?"

"It's been almost three months now," her voice trailed off.

"Gone .. like ...?"

"Yes."

"But I told him I would be there for him." I protested.

"We didn't know how to contact you," she explained. "We didn't know what happened to you after you left Boulder."

"Oh, no, I'm so sorry," I didn't know what to say. How can anyone possibly know what to say? "I'm so sorry. So very ...

She breathed in. "Some days are better than others." She breathed out.

When I put down the receiver, I was alone.

I hadn't kept my promise to Gary and now it was too late and I was alone.

All alone. In the wilderness. Darkness everywhere.

And I couldn't do anything about it. There was nothing I could do – ever – to make up for my broken promise. No matter how much I wished or ached. No matter how much it hurt. No matter how many times, or how many ways, I tried to work out how things might have turned out differently. There was no possible way in heaven or on earth to ever bring it all back. There was nothing I – or anyone – could ever do about it.

Some things can never be undone.

Gary and my magic ticket had both gone out into the universe and no longer existed as separate things, except in my memories. And someday – soon enough – I would follow. Someday. Not yet, but someday. I was going to be just ...

Gone.

Forever.

And that was the easy part.

The much harder part was what to do until then.

I didn't know what I was going to become of me in the meantime.

Or what I was going to do.

But I was going ...

Just going.

Gary couldn't help me.

Mom and Dad couldn't help me.

The Mormon Church couldn't help me.

There weren't any rules anymore.

No requirements either.

The rest was up to me.

I put on Gary's favorite record and turned it up loud.

"I sat looking 'round. I looked at my face in the mirror."

When Side-One finished, I flipped the record over and played Side-Two.

And when that was over, I stood up and introduced myself.

To myself.

"Meet the new boss."`

Then I picked up my guitar and played.

Epilogue
Guaranteed to Bleed
Music & Lyrics by Dallas Doctor
©2011 Wild Moose Music (BMI)

(Verse 1)
In my Bleeding Madras shirt
And button-fly 501s
I stepped out onto the stage
My journey had begun
I sang World Without Love
Made her turn her head
The prettiest girl in the room
Turned to me and said

She said

(Chorus)
You'll never get everything you want
You already have all that you need
If you get lucky
There'll be moments of magic
But you're Guaranteed to Bleed

(Verse 2)
Sometimes, to get along
It's tempting not to say it
He saw it on the set list
Told us not to play it
We couldn't get permission
He told us to obey
But it was Blowin' in the Wind
So we played it anyway

Because

(Chorus)
    You'll never get everything you want
    You already have all that you need
    If you get lucky
    There'll be moments of magic
    But you're Guaranteed to Bleed

(Verse 3)
So we set out on the road
With our songs to see the world
We didn't see much
But we sure did see some girls
Nights under the lights
Playin' loud and keepin' score
If I could do it different
I'd only do it more
                        But

(Chorus)
    You'll never get everything you want
    You already have all that you need
    If you get lucky
    There'll be moments of magic
    But you're Guaranteed to Bleed

(Bridge)
There will be stones unturned
There will be songs unsung
There will be promises broken
And deeds undone
There will be bitter disappointments
And dreams overdue
We rarely recognize them
When they do come true

(Verse 4)
Now my Bleeding Madras shirt
Is hangin' on the wall
Between the miles and the memories
The ones I recall
But I remember what she said
Her words of wisdom came to pass
Tonight, to all you dreamers
I raise my glass
                    And sing:

(Chorus)
    You'll never get everything you want
    You already have all that you need
    If you get lucky
    There'll be moments of magic
    But you're Guaranteed to Bleed

ABOUT THE AUTHOR

Age 5 – at home in Idaho

Age 59 – at home in New York City

Dallas Doctor lives in Midtown Manhattan, writes songs & stories about the meaning of life, plays piano & guitar, and runs the Boston Marathon every April.

Next:

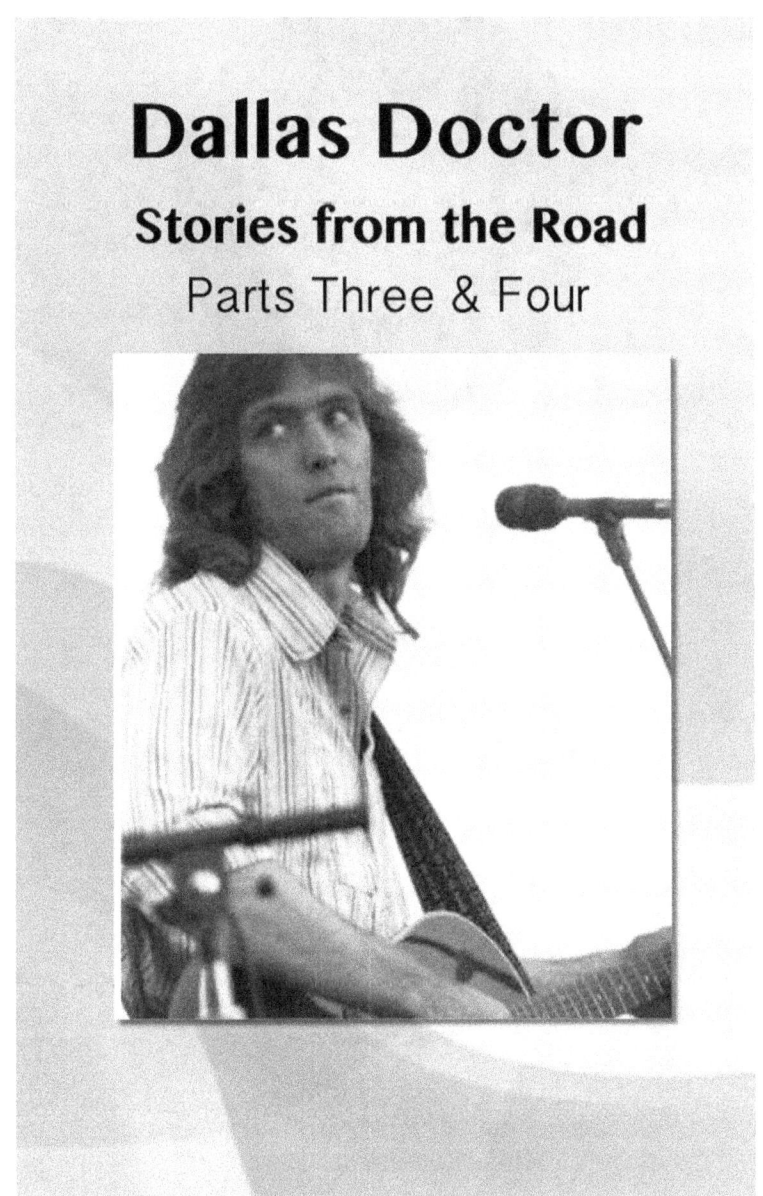

Dallas Doctor
Stories from the Road
Parts Three & Four

ALSO AVAILABLE FROM TRUFFLE PRESS

www.trufflepress.com

7" Vinyl (45rpm)
Side A: Heart of Darkness
Side B: Guaranteed to Bleed

7" Vinyl (45rpm)
Side A: Fire in my Heart
Side B: For Your Love

ALSO AVAILABLE FROM TRUFFLE PRESS

www.trufflepress.com

The Book of Bo
Bo
132 pages (nonfiction)

Abandoned
Bo
252 pages (fiction)

god's favorite band
Dallas Doctor
192 pages (fiction)

~

Vinyl/CDs/mp3s

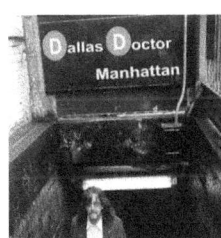

Manhattan
Dallas Doctor
Full Album (11 songs)

Goin' Blind
The Amazing Idiots
Full Album (12 songs)

By the Numbers
Dallas Doctor
Full Album (10 songs)

~

More available at
www.dockity.com

www.ingramcontent.com/pod-product-compliance
Lightning Source LLC
Chambersburg PA
CBHW070309260626
47160CB00003B/786